PROLOGUE

St. Moritz—February 2017

A 1946 MACALLAN, his three closest friends consuming that exceptional bottle of whiskey with him and a game of high-stakes poker played in a private room at one of St. Moritz's swankiest clubs was a trifecta of such absolute perfection, Alejandro Salazar could not deny it was the ideal ending to a day spent paraskiing in the Swiss Alps.

Cutting a vertical line to the cliff's edge, throwing yourself off a mountainside only to hope your parachute landed you in an equally traversable stretch of snow below required some coming down from—quality bonding time that only this particular male ritual could supply.

It had dwindled down to the four of them tonight after today's challenge—Sebastien Atkinson, his good friend and mentor, founder of the extreme sports club they'd joined in college; Antonio Di Marcello, a giant in the global construction industry and Stavros Xenakis, the soon-to-be CEO of Dynami Pharmaceutical—perhaps the only quartet with the spare change to put up the ante this type of a game required.

Not even the trio of delectable Scandinavian women draped across the packed bar, looking for an opportunity to crash their party had been enticement enough to abandon such a rich moment in time. Friendships forged in fire.

Just last year they had pulled Sebastien off a Himalayan mountainside before it had collapsed in a cloud of snow that had nearly killed them all. The ending to this weekend's challenge seemed tame in comparison.

An intense feeling of well-being settling over him, Alejandro sat back in his chair, rested his tumbler on his thigh and considered the table. There was a different air about the celebration tonight—subtle, but distinct.

Perhaps last year's near tragedy still lay too close to the surface. Perhaps it had reminded them all that their club mantra—life is short—was truer than it had ever been. Or maybe it was because Sebastien had gone and done the sacrilegious in getting married, taking the sampling of the popular ski enclave's wares off the table.

Stavros, as if sensing this new playing field, eyed Sebastien across the table. "How's your wife?" he asked with a curl of his lips.

"Better company than you. Why so surly tonight?"

Stavros grimaced. "I haven't won yet." He lifted a shoulder. "And my grandfather is threatening to disinherit me if I don't marry soon. I'd tell him to go to hell, but…"

"Your mother," Alejandro said.

"Exactly."

The Greek billionaire was between a rock and a hard place. If he didn't play the game, extend the Xenakis line with an heir, his grandfather would follow through on his threat to disinherit Stavros before he assumed control of the pharmaceutical empire that would be his.

Stavros would have called his bluff, walked away with pleasure if it weren't for his mother and sisters who would be stripped of everything they possessed if that happened, something Stavros would never allow.

Sebastien pushed a pile of chips toward the center of the table. "Do you ever get the feeling we spend too much of our lives counting our money and chasing superficial thrills at the expense of something more meaningful?"

Antonio tossed a handful of chips at Alejandro. "You called it," his friend muttered, "four drinks and he's already philosophizing."

Sebastien scowled at Stavros as he added his own chips

Alejandro cradled the glass in his palm, a ghost of a smile curving his lips.

"I do care, Cecily. Hence the situation we find ourselves in. I told you that before I knew about the pregnancy. In fact everything I said to you in Kentucky was true, every emotion I expressed real. The only thing I lied about was my identity, and that I had to do."

Her stomach curled with the need to believe him. To believe *something* in all this was true and real—that what they'd shared had been real. But she'd be a fool to take what he was saying at face value—even more of a fool than she'd already been.

He gestured toward the cream sofa that faced the spectacular view. "Why don't we sit down?"

"I'd prefer to stand."

"Fine." He lowered himself onto the chaise, splaying his long legs out in front of him. "We are keeping this baby, Cecily."

"Of course we are. *I* am," she corrected. "I would never do anything else."

"Good. And just to clarify," he drawled, eyes on hers, "when I said *we* are keeping this baby I meant *us*. We are *both* going to be parents to this child, which means we need to be *together*."

She frowned. "What do you mean *together*?"

"I mean we will marry."

Her knees went weak. She slid down onto the sofa, a buzzing sound filling her ears. "You can't be serious."

"Oh,

'I'll wager that not one of you can go two weeks without your credit cards...'

The Secret Billionaires

*Challenged to go undercover—
but tempted to blow it all!*

Tycoons Antonio Di Marcello,
Stavros Xenakis and Alejandro Salazar
cannot imagine life without their decadent wealth,
incredible power and untouchable status—but
neither can they resist their competitive natures!

Dared to abandon all they know,
these extraordinary men leave behind their
billionaire lifestyles and take on 'ordinary' lives.

But, disguised as a mechanic, a pool boy and a
groom, they're about to meet the *real* challenge...

Conquering the women they'll meet along the way!

SALAZAR'S
ONE-NIGHT HEIR

BY
JENNIFER HAYWARD

MILLS
& BOON

First Published in Great Britain 2017
By Mills & Boon, an imprint of HarperCollins*Publishers*
1 London Bridge Street, London, SE1 9GF

© 2017 Jennifer Drogell

ISBN: 978-0-263-92449-7

Printed and bound in Spain
by CPI, Barcelona

Jennifer Hayward has been a fan of romance since filching her sister's novels to escape her teenage angst. Her career in journalism and PR, including years of working alongside powerful, charismatic CEOs and travelling the world, has provided perfect fodder for the fast-paced, sexy stories she likes to write—always with a touch of humour. A native of Canada's East Coast, Jennifer lives in Toronto with her Viking husband and young Viking-in-training.

Books by Jennifer Hayward

Mills & Boon Modern Romance

A Debt Paid in the Marriage Bed
The Magnate's Manifesto
Changing Constantinou's Game

The Billionaire's Legacy

A Deal for the Di Sione Ring

Kingdoms & Crowns

Carrying the King's Pride
Claiming the Royal Innocent
Marrying Her Royal Enemy

The Tenacious Tycoons

Tempted by Her Billionaire Boss
Reunited for the Billionaire's Legacy

Society Weddings

The Italian's Deal for I Do

The Delicious De Campos

The Divorce Party
An Exquisite Challenge
The Truth About De Campo

Visit the Author Profile page at millsandboon.co.uk for more titles.

For my husband, Johan,
who helped me find my perfect ending in a book
that stole my heart. You call life with a writer a
'rollercoaster' but I think you secretly like it!

For Melita and Maria—your help with the beautiful
Portuguese language was so very much appreciated.

And for my co-writers Dani Collins and
Rachael Thomas—it was a joy to work together
and create such a fabulous series.
I can't wait for the world to read it!

XX

to Alejandro's pile. The Greek billionaire shrugged. "I said three. My losing streak continues."

"I'm serious." Sebastien eyed the table. "At our level, it's numbers on a page. Points on a scoreboard. What does it contribute to our lives? Money doesn't buy happiness."

"It buys some pretty nice substitutes," Antonio interjected.

Sebastien's mouth twisted. "Like your cars?" he mused, then moved his gaze to Alejandro. "Your private island? You don't even use that boat you're so proud of," he said, moving on to Stavros. "We buy expensive toys and play dangerous games, but does it enrich our lives? Feed our souls?"

"Exactly what are you suggesting?" Alejandro drawled, pushing a pile of chips into the pot. "We go live with the Buddhists in the mountains? Learn the meaning of life? Renounce our worldly possessions to find inner clarity?"

Sebastien made a sound at the back of his throat. "You three couldn't go two weeks without your wealth and family names to support you. Your gilded existence makes you blind to reality."

Alejandro stiffened. He took offence to that. Sebastien might be the only self-made man among them, older than the rest by three years, but they had all achieved success in their own right.

Leading his family company had been Alejandro's birthright, yes, but *he* had been the one to transform the Salazar Coffee Company from a fledgling international player into a global household name as CEO. He had *more* than paid his dues.

Stavros threw away three cards. "Try telling us you would go back to when you were broke, before you made your fortune. Hungry isn't happy. That's why you're such a rich bastard now."

"As it happens," Sebastien countered with a deceptively

casual shrug, "I've been thinking of donating half my fortune to charity to start a global search and rescue fund. Not everyone has friends who will dig him out of an avalanche with their bare hands."

Alejandro almost choked on the sip of whiskey he'd taken. "Are you serious? That's what? Five billion?"

"You can't take it with you. I'll tell you what," Sebastien mused, gaze moving from one to the other, "you three manage to go two weeks without your credit cards and family name and I'll do it."

Silence fell over the table. "Starting when?" Alejandro queried. "We all have responsibilities."

"Fair enough," Sebastien agreed. "Clear the decks at home. But be prepared for word from me—and two weeks in the real world."

Alejandro blinked. "You're really going to wager half your fortune on a cakewalk of a challenge?"

"If you'll put up your island…your favorite toys? Yes." Sebastien lifted his whiskey glass. "I say where and when."

"Easy," said Stavros. "Count me in."

They all clinked glasses, Alejandro dismissing the challenge as one of Sebastien's philosophical, whiskey-induced rants.

Until he ended up undercover as a groom in the Hargroves' legendary Kentucky stables exactly five months later.

CHAPTER ONE

Five months later—Esmerelda, the Hargrove Estate, Kentucky. Day one of Alejandro's challenge

CECILY HARGROVE TOOK the turn to the final line of jumps at such a tight angle, Bacchus's hind end spun out before her horse regained his balance, smoothed out his stride and headed toward the first oxer.

Too slow. Way too slow. Dammit, what was wrong with him?

She dug her heels into her horse's sides, pushing him forward to give them the momentum they needed for the jump, but Bacchus's hesitancy at takeoff threw their timing all off—only her horse's pure physical power allowing them to clear the fence.

Jaw set, frustration surging through her, she finished the last two jumps of the combination, then brought Bacchus to a dancing trot, then a walk, halting in front of her trainer.

Dale gave her a grim look as she pulled off her hat, the hot summer sun sticking the strands of her hair to her head. Her stomach knotted. "I don't want to know."

"Sixty-eight seconds. You need to figure out what's wrong with that horse, Cecily."

Tell her something she didn't know. With her second mount, Derringer, showing his inexperience in competition, Bacchus was her only chance to make this year's world championship team. Fully healed from their accident last year, her horse was physically sound, it was his mental outlook she was worried about.

If she didn't straighten out his head—this strange hesitancy he was displaying toward jumps he never used to blink at—her dream would be sunk before it had even started.

The only thing in this world that meant anything to her.

"Do it again," Dale instructed.

She shook her head, fury and frustration welling up inside her to spur a wet heat at the back of her eyes. "I'm done."

"Cec—"

She kicked Bacchus into a canter and headed for the barn, fighting back the tears. She had handled all the lemons life had thrown at her and Lord knew there had been a few of them, but *this*, this was not something she could fail at. Not when she'd spent every waking moment since she was five working toward this day.

Pulling Bacchus to a halt in front of the groom who stood lounging against the stable door, she slid off and threw the reins at him with more force than she'd intended. He caught them with a lithe movement, pushing away from the door. Hands clenched at her sides, she spun on her heel and turned to leave.

"You don't cool your horse down?"

The unfamiliar low, slightly accented drawl stopped her in her tracks. Spinning around, she took in its owner. The new groom she'd seen with Cliff earlier, presumably. She'd been so preoccupied she hadn't paid any attention to him. She wondered now how that had been possible.

Tall, well over six feet, he was pure, packed muscle in the T-shirt and jeans he wore. Slowly, furiously, she slid her gaze up that impressive body and found the rest of him was equally jaw dropping. His black hair was worn at a slightly rebellious length, days-old stubble lined a brutally handsome, square-cut jaw, his eyes the most sinfully dark ones she'd ever seen.

Her stomach flip flopped, a moment of sizzling hot, sexual chemistry arcing between them. She allowed herself to sink into it for a moment, to absorb the shimmer way down low, because it was something she hadn't felt in a long, long time, *if ever.*

His blatant stare didn't waver. Unnerved by the intensity of the connection, she sliced it dead. "You're new," she said icily, lifting her chin. "What's your name?"

A dip of his head. "Colt Banyon, ma'am. At your service."

She nodded. "I'm fairly sure then, *Colt*, that Cliff will have explained the finer points of your job to you?"

"He did."

"Why then, do you think it's okay to question how I handle my horse?"

He lifted a shoulder. "It seems to me you were having some trouble out there today. In my experience, spending some bonding time with your mount can help with the trust factor."

The pressure in her head threatened to explode through her skull. *No one dared talk to her like that.* She couldn't believe his audacity.

She took a step closer, discovering just how big he was when she had to tip her head back to look up at him, his dangerously beautiful eyes a rich whiskey fire lighting an inky black canvas.

"And from *which* school of psychobabble does that assessment come from?"

His sensual mouth curved. "My grandmother. She's a magician with horses."

The smile might have taken her breath away if the red haze creeping across her brain hadn't taken complete hold of her now. "How about this, *Colt*?" she suggested, voice dripping with disdain. "The next time you or your grandmother achieves a top one hundred world cup ranking, you can tell me how to handle my horse. Until then, how about you keep your mouth shut and do your job?"

His beautiful eyes widened.

She winced inwardly. *Had she really just said that?*

Shocked at her loss of control, fighting desperately to find some, she clutched her fingers tight around her hat. "He's recovering from torn ligaments on his rear hind leg," she said, nodding toward Bacchus. "Keep an eye on it."

Alejandro watched Cecily Hargrove flounce off, hat in hand, convinced the tiny blonde would be the thing that tested his control in this challenge Sebastien had issued him.

She'd been raising hell around the barn all morning. He was simply the latest in a long list of casualties.

Mucking out stalls, breaking his back caring for thirty horses, twelve hours a day would be child's play compared to dealing with *that* piece of work. She had a mouth on her that would strip the paint off a car and an attitude to match.

Unfortunately, he conceded, studying her fine rear end in the tight-fitting gray breeches as she stalked away, she was also extraordinarily beautiful. Traffic-stoppingly, outrageously beautiful. He would have had to have been fixed like half the horses in the barn not to have appreciated the delicate, heart-shaped face, remarkable blue eyes and honey blond hair that gave her an almost angelic look. Highly deceptive, clearly.

Blowing out a breath, he gathered up Bacchus's reins and took the beautiful bay gelding for a walk along the cobblestoned laneway to cool him off. To cool *himself* off.

It had been damn near impossible to swallow the comeback that had risen to his lips when Cecily Hargrove had thrown her world cup ranking at him. His grandmother had been top three in the world. She would have ridden circles around the superior *Ms. Hargrove* in her day. But exposing his true identity as a Salazar and rendering this challenge null and void wasn't something he could do. Not when Antonio and Stavros had already successfully completed theirs.

Not when his private island in the BVI was up for grabs—one of the few places on earth he found peace.

He led a cooled-down Bacchus into the barn and rubbed him down with a cloth. The therapeutic work he'd always loved gave him a chance to process the last, bizarre, twenty-four hours of his life.

It had not surprised him when Sebastien's jet had deposited him at the Louisville airport last night where he'd been instructed to report to the Hargroves' legendary, hundred-acre horse farm just outside of the city. Nor to find in the rustic cabin he'd been allocated in the staff quarters a couple of pairs of jeans, some T-shirts and boots, as well as a small stack of cash and an ancient mobile phone. It was exactly the same picture that had greeted Antonio and Stavros upon their arrival at their challenges.

The cryptic note that had been left on top of the pile of clothes had been similar as well.

For the next two weeks Alejandro Salazar does not exist. You are now Colt Banyon, talented drifter groom. You will report to Cliff Taylor at the stables at six a.m. tomorrow, where you will work for the next two weeks.

You will not break your cover under any circumstance. The only communication you may have with the outside world is with your fellow challenge-takers on the phone provided.

Why this particular assignment for you? I know you have been searching for the time to provide your grandmother with the proof she desires to right a wrong long-ago perpetrated. To restore the Salazar family honor. Your time as a groom will provide you

with both the means and the opportunity to do so.
I hope it offers you the closure you are looking for.
*   I wish you luck. Don't blow this, Alejandro. I've*
gone to a great deal of effort to provide you with an
airtight identity. If you, Antonio and Stavros success-
fully complete your assignments, I will donate half
of my fortune, as promised, to setting up a global
search and rescue team. It will save many more lives.
Sebastien

Alejandro's mouth twisted as he switched to Bacchus's other side, toweling the sweat from the gelding's dark coat. No doubt the idea of him breaking his back shoveling horse manure for two weeks with a name torn from the pages of a Hollywood script had provided an endless source of amusement for his mentor. But if Sebastien had been here, he would have told him this chance to provide his grandmother with the justice she was seeking was exactly the kind of closure he'd been looking for.

The feud between the Salazars and Hargroves had been going on for decades—ever since Quinton Hargrove had illegally bred his mare Demeter to his grandmother, Adriana Salazar's, prize stallion Diablo while the horse had been on loan to an American breeder. The Hargroves had gone on to build an entire show jumping legacy around Diablo's bloodline, one Adriana had never been able to match.

Heartbroken, his grandmother had been unable to attain proof as to what the Hargroves had done, watching as her fortunes plummeted and the Hargroves' star had risen. Sebastien, in setting up the elaborate identity he had for him had put Alejandro in the perfect position to acquire that proof. Not only did he have the skills to carry out the subterfuge from summers and holidays spent on his grandmother's Belgian horse farm, he had her touch with a horse.

He ran the towel down Bacchus's hind end. Somehow,

he acknowledged, it seemed almost *too* simple, this assignment of his, given the emotionally complex challenges Antonio and Stavros had been handed.

Antonio had been sent undercover to work as a mechanic at a garage in Milan. No issue there given his skill with a wrench. Far more shocking had been the child the Greek billionaire had discovered, the product of an old love affair. Antonio was still grappling with the considerable fallout of that life-altering discovery.

Stavros had warily gone next, finding himself sent to Greece to pose as a pool boy at his old family villa, a place he had long given a wide berth. Purchased by new owners, the property still held the ghosts of Stavros's childhood, the site of his father's death in a boating accident in which Stavros had survived.

Which undoubtedly left Alejandro the winner in the challenge lottery. Collecting a DNA sample from Bacchus, Cecily Hargrove's prize horse, to prove the Hargroves' crime was as simple as saving a few mane hairs from a brush and sending them off to Stavros to analyze in one of his high-tech labs.

Which left his biggest challenge to find a way to steer clear of Ms. Cecily Hargrove's razor-sharp mouth and perfect behind over the next two weeks.

Cecily's bad behavior plagued her all afternoon and well into dinner in the formal dining room at Esmerelda, a ridiculous indulgence on her stepmother's part when the stately redbrick manor's elegant, columned entertaining space seated thirty and it was only she, her father and her stepmother dining tonight.

She spent most of the insufferably dry meal staring moodily out the window. Her mother, Zara, had raised her to have impeccable manners. She was *never* rude. But Colt Banyon had hit a nerve this afternoon—a guilt she'd been harboring perhaps. A part of her knew this mess with Bacchus wasn't just his fault—that whatever had happened to them in that horrific accident in London was something that still haunted them both.

Dessert was finally served. Her stepmother, Kay, otherwise known as the Wicked Witch of the South, flicked a jasmine-scented wrist at her as a maid served a lime sorbet. "What are you wearing to the party next week?"

Something her stepmother would undoubtedly hate on sight.

"I don't know," she dismissed. "I'll find something."

Kay eyed her. "You know Knox Henderson is coming here specifically to court you. He's number forty-two on the Forbes list, Cecily. A catch if there ever was one."

Her lip curled. "No one uses the word 'court' anymore. And like I've told you a half a dozen times before, I have no interest in Knox."

"Why not?"

Because he was an arrogant jerk who owned half of Texas with his massive cattle ranches and oil reserves, merely looking for a wife to decorate his salon in entertainment magazine photo spreads. Because he reminded her far too much of her ex, Davis—another male who'd been far too rich and far too appreciative of multiple members of the opposite sex—*all at the same time.*

"I am not marrying him." She lifted her chin and stared her stepmother down. "End of story. Stop matchmaking. It's only going to be embarrassing for both of us if you keep this up."

"Perhaps Cecily is right," her father interjected, sweeping his cool, gray gaze over her. "She would do better to focus on the task at hand. Dale said your times today were still subpar. Do I need to buy you another horse to make this happen?"

Her stomach twisted. No, 'I'm sorry you had such a bad

day, honey.' No 'You've got what it takes, just stick with it' from her father. Never any of that. Only the stern, silver-haired disapproval that was her father's de facto response. It made her feel about two feet tall.

Her lashes lowered. "I don't have time to break in a new horse, Daddy. Besides, the committee will expect me on Bacchus."

"Then what do we need to do?"

"I will figure it out."

Suddenly the idea of Knox Henderson's impending visit combined with the vast amount of pressure being heaped on her from all directions vaporized any desire for dessert.

She set her spoon down with a clatter. "If you'll excuse me, I have a headache. I think I'll go lie down."

"Cecily."

Her stepmother put a hand on her father's arm. "Let her go. You know what she's like when she's in one of these moods."

Cecily ignored her, scraping back her chair and leaving with a click of her heels on the hardwood floor. She started toward her bedroom, then changed her mind, taking a detour to the kitchen where she acquired some of Bacchus's favorite breakfast cereal, then headed out the back door to the barn.

She thought she might owe both Bacchus and Colt Banyon an apology. She told herself that was the only reason she was venturing out into a balmy, perfect Kentucky evening when she had a stack of entrance forms waiting to be filled out. It was not, she assured herself, because of Colt Banyon's sinful dark eyes she couldn't forget.

Her bad timing on the course earlier today seemed to follow her as she entered the barn to find the grooms had finished up work. Not about to track Colt Banyon down at the staff quarters, she headed for Bacchus's box.

She pulled up short when she got there, watching with

astonishment as her horse, extremely picky when it came to grooms and highly nerved, blew out a breath and closed his eyes, putty under Colt's hands as the groom massaged his head. She hadn't seen him look this relaxed since before the accident.

Her attention shifted to the two-footed male in the box. Still clad in the close-fitting faded jeans, a gray T-shirt skimming his amazing abs, she found herself transfixed by the ripple of muscle in his powerful arms...by the lean, taut, undeniably ogle-worthy thighs underneath the worn denim.

He was a *man*—unlike Knox Henderson who preferred to preen like a peacock, there was a quiet substance to Colt that held her in its thrall.

He slid his hands down her horse's head and began working his neck muscles, the kneading movement of his big hands making her horse shudder. Her stomach curled, tiny pinpricks of heat unfolding beneath her skin.

Would he handle a woman with such sensual precision? What would those hands feel like? Would they be deliberate and demanding? Slow and seductive? *All of the above?*

Bacchus lifted his head, his soft nicker of welcome causing the subject of her fascination to turn around. She wiped her expression clean, but perhaps not quick enough. Colt Banyon's cool, dark stare made her freeze, utterly disconcerted.

"Why aren't you eating with the others?" she blurted out.

A blast of arctic air directed her way. "Wasn't hungry."

She sank her hands into her pockets. Blew out a breath. "I owe you an apology for my behavior earlier. I was frustrated, I took it out on you. I'm sorry."

A barely perceptible blink of those long, dark lashes. "Apology accepted."

He turned and went back to work. Her skin burned.

He'd clearly formed an opinion of her and wasn't about to change it. Which should have been fine because she was used to people forming false impressions of her. Sometimes she even encouraged it, because it was easier than trying to maintain human relationships, something that never seemed to work out for her.

But for some reason, she wanted Colt Banyon to approve of her. Maybe because her horse had already given him the thumbs up and Bacchus's opinion was never wrong.

Her horse nuzzled the pocket of her dress. She pulled out a handful of his favorite brightly colored fruit breakfast cereal and fed it to him.

Colt eyed her hand. "What is *that?*"

"Breakfast of champions. He'll do anything for it."

"Except jump the course the way you want him to."

Ouch. She winced at the dig. "Are you always this—"

"Impertinent?"

"I didn't say that."

"But you thought it."

"I *think,*" she corrected stiffly, "that you are direct. And that you don't like me very much."

He glanced at her, face impassive. "It doesn't matter what I think. I'm paid to follow orders just like you said."

She bit her lip. "I didn't mean that."

"Sure you did."

Wow. He wasn't going to make this easy for her. She watched as he ran his hand over Bacchus's side and dug his fingers into his trapezoids, key muscles her horse used to balance himself with. "What are you doing?"

"He seemed stiff when you rode him earlier. I thought a massage might loosen him up."

"Did your grandmother teach you that too?"

"Yes. If he's tight, he can't stretch over the jumps properly."

Well she knew that, of course. Jumping was all about form. But she'd only ever heard of equine therapists doing this kind of a massage.

"Is your grandmother a therapist?"

He shook his head. "Just a horse lover with a special touch."

"Does she live in New Mexico?"

A longer glance at her this time. "You been checking my résumé out?"

Heat stained her cheeks. "I like to know who's working in my stables."

"So you can see which 'school of psychobabble' we come from?"

"Colt—"

He started working on her horse's back. She crossed her arms over her chest and leaned back against the stall. "We had an accident," she said quietly. "In London last year. Something in the crowd spooked Bacchus as we approached a combination. His takeoff was all wrong—we crashed through the fence."

She closed her eyes as the sickening thud, still so clear, so horrifically real, reverberated in her head. "I was lucky I didn't break my neck. I broke my collarbone and arm instead. Bacchus tore tendons—badly. Physically, he's a hundred percent but mentally he hasn't been right since then. That's why I was so frustrated today."

He turned around and leaned against the wall. The corded muscles in his forearms flexed as he folded them over his chest, a flicker of something she couldn't read sliding across his cool, even gaze. "That had to have left some emotional dents in you as well."

She nodded. "I thought I was over it. Maybe I'm not."

Alejandro knew he should keep up the brush off signals until Cecily Hargrove walked back out that door—the safest place for her. But there was a fragility that radiated from her tonight, dark emotional bruises in her eyes he couldn't ignore. Perhaps they were from the accident. He thought they might be from a hell of a lot further back.

His heart tugged. Her undeniably beautiful face, bare of makeup, blue summer dress the same vibrant shade as her eyes, she looked exceedingly young and vulnerable. His grandmother had always said showjumping was a mental game. If you lost your edge, it all fell apart. Maybe Cecily had lost hers.

"Maybe you need to take a step back," he suggested. "Take some time for you and Bacchus to fully heal—mentally and physically. Figure out what's missing."

She shook her head. "I don't have time. I have a big event in a month. If I don't perform in the top three there I won't make the world championship team. Bacchus is the only horse I have that's at that level."

"So you make it next year."

"That's not an option."

"Why not?" He frowned. "What are you—mid-twenties? You have all the time in the world to make the team."

Her mouth twisted. "Not when you're a Hargrove, you don't. My grandmother and mother were on the team. I am *expected* to make it. If I don't, it will be a huge disappointment."

"To who?"

"My father. My coach. The team. Everyone who's backed me. They've spent a fortune in time and money to get me here."

That he understood. He'd spent a lifetime trying to live up to his own legacy—to the destiny that had been handed to him from the first day he could walk. Sent to an elite boarding school in America from his native Brazil when he was six, then on to Harvard, the pressure had been relentless.

When he'd moved to New York to run the Salazar Coffee Company's global operations as the company's CEO, that pressure had escalated to a whole other level, driven by a ferociously competitive international marketplace and a father who had never been content with less than a hundred and ten percent from his sons.

He knew how that pressure could rule your life. How it could crush your soul if you let it.

He set his gaze on the woman in front of him. "You know better than anyone what you do is as much psychology as it is sport. Master the course in your head and you're halfway there. Fail to do so and you're dead in the water." He shook his head. "If you push Bacchus before you're both ready, it could end up in an even worse disaster than the one you've already been through."

Long, golden-tipped lashes shaded her eyes. Chewing on her lip, she studied him for a long moment. "Was your grandmother a show jumper?"

Meu Deus. He gave himself a mental slap for revealing that much. He'd thought it an innocent enough reference at the time with Ms. High and Mighty goading him, but it had clearly been a stupid thing to do. Proof he liked to live close to the edge.

"She competed in small, regional stuff," he backpedalled. "Nothing at your level. She gave it up to have a family. But she had a way with horses like no one I've ever seen."

Her expressive eyes took on a reflective cast. "My mama was like that. Horses gravitated to her—it was like she spoke their language. They'd do anything for her in the ring."

Zara Hargrove. Alejandro knew from his grandmother she had died in a riding accident at the height of her career. Which would have made Cecily only a teenager when she'd lost her... *Tough.*

He ran a palm over the stubble on his jaw, hardening his heart against those dark bruised eyes. "You will figure this out. Bacchus will come around."

Her lips pursed. "I hope so."

She fed Bacchus another handful of cereal. He pulled his gaze away from the vulnerable curve of her mouth. *Dio. She was the enemy.* It might be guilt by association, she might have been *trained* to be a Hargrove, but she was one nonetheless. He was nuts to be standing here trying to solve her problems.

He knelt beside Bacchus's hind leg. "Show me where he tore the tendons."

She squatted beside him and ran her hand down the horse's leg. "Here."

"Difficult spot." He wrapped his fingers around the tendons and very gently worked the leg, massaging the sinewy flesh until it eased beneath his fingers.

"Can I try?" Cecily asked.

He nodded and dropped his hand.

She wrapped her fingers around the horse's leg, kneading his flesh. But her touch was too tentative, too light to do any good.

"Like this." He closed his fingers over hers to demonstrate, increasing the pressure. The warmth of her hand bled into his, a fission of electricity passing between them. Heat flared beneath his skin. Her breath grew shallow. He inhaled her delicate floral scent, so soft and seductive as it infiltrated his senses with potent effect. They may have had a rocky start, she might be the enemy, but his body wasn't registering either of those facts, consumed with a sensual awareness of her that clawed at his skin.

She turned to look at him, eyes darkening. "Have you ever thought of doing this for a living? You're very good at it."

"I've thought about it." He responded as Colt Banyon,

professional drifter. "But I like to travel too much. Maybe someday I'll settle down and get my own place."

She didn't scoff at that, as if he didn't have a hope in hell of ever owning a place like this. Didn't know he could buy and sell her family ten times over. Only said quietly, sincerity shining in her eyes, "I hope you do that someday. You'd be amazing at it."

He thought then that perhaps first impressions hadn't done Cecily Hargrove justice. That if he curved his fingers around her neck and drew her to him for a kiss so he could taste that delectable mouth, she wouldn't protest, she'd meet him halfway. That if he did, he might be able to banish some of those dark shadows from her eyes for just a few minutes.

Why all of a sudden it was the most unbearably tempting proposition when it was the last thing in the world he should ever do was beyond him.

He pushed to his feet before madness ensued. "A few minutes of that every day will help him stretch out, trust himself a bit more. It might help."

She rose to her feet beside him, any hint of an invitation gone from those blue eyes. If he saw a flash of regret there, she masked it just as quickly.

"Thank you, Colt," she said quietly, brushing her palms against her dress. "He's in excellent hands. Y'all have yourself a good night."

Oh, my God. Cecily dragged in a deep breath as she exited the stables on weak knees, the earth feeling as if it was shifting beneath her feet. *What had just happened?*

You didn't invite a complete stranger to kiss you when he'd clearly barely been tolerating your presence and didn't even *like* you. And yet, her dazed brain processed, for a second there, she'd thought he'd been thinking about kissing her too before he'd replaced those barriers of his and put her back in her place as surely as she'd put him in his earlier today.

Had she imagined it?

She pressed her palms to her heated cheeks. She shouldn't be interested in kissing *anyone* right now. It was the last thing she should be doing with her career hanging in the balance.

Skirting the floodlit natural water grotto her father had spent millions building for her mother, she took the path to the house. Perhaps she should go stick her head in *there*. It might inject some sense into her.

Hadn't her disastrous engagement to Davis taught her a lesson? Good looking men were trouble. A disaster waiting to happen. She was better off sticking with males of the four legged variety. They never broke her heart.

CHAPTER TWO

CECILY SPENT THE next few days steadfastly ignoring sexy, elusive Colt Banyon and putting all her focus into her practice sessions. But it seemed the harder she tried, the worse her times became—as if desperation was setting in and Bacchus could sense it, feeding off her nerves in all the worst ways.

By the time Friday rolled around, her event three weeks away, she was at her wit's end. She could continue to pound away at the fruitless efforts that were getting her nowhere or she could follow Colt's suggestion and take a step back.

She couldn't afford to give up on her hopes for the season, but perhaps she might be able to rewire her horse's brain with a total change of pace. Maybe Bacchus just needed a mental breather, an escape from the pressure cooker. *Just like her.*

An idea filled her head over tea in the thankfully deserted breakfast room. Except she knew her father wouldn't allow it unless she took someone with her and since having company along for the ride defeated the purpose of obtaining some peace, it wasn't an option.

Unless she took the less than talkative Colt with her, she mused over a sip of tea. She could pick his brain about some of his techniques along the way. While keeping her head in sane territory, of course, something that shouldn't be hard because Colt would clearly give her the brush off again if she did something dumb like invite him to kiss her, which of course, she wouldn't.

Her mouth curved. It was a plan. She finished her tea, collected her things and went off to execute.

* * *

Alejandro dropped the package off at the courier office in town on his mid-morning break. Containing a sample of Bacchus's mane hairs, it was now up to Stavros's high tech lab to confirm the Hargroves' crime.

He texted Stavros from the truck.

Package has been sent. Obrigado amigo, I owe you one.

Forget it. I'm feeling generous. I am, after all, soon to be a married man.

Alejandro almost dropped his phone.

Sorry?

You heard me. Details to come. Got to run.

Got to run? Alejandro eyed the phone as he threw it on the seat of the truck. *Antonio with an insta-family? Stavros married?* What the hell was going on? It was… *insano.*

Stavros, he bemusedly processed as he started the truck, didn't even sound panicked about it. He sounded almost… *cheerful.*

The sense of relief he'd been feeling about having netted this particular challenge magnified ten-fold as he drove back to the farm. No chance of any of those emotional attachments with him. He didn't need to acquire a wife as Stavros did, had no undiscovered children lying around—he'd made sure of that. And Sebastien knew his feelings on marriage.

When the day came for him to make a match to deliver the Salazar heir, it would be at least a few years down the road with a woman he'd handpicked as a sensible selection. He would research her just as he would an expensive car, making sure she ticked all the right boxes for the rational, practical match he had planned. Because he knew from personal history, impulse purchases, matches made out of passion never lasted. His parents were a perfect example of that.

He reached the stables five minutes after his break officially ended. Putting his mind blowing conversation with Stavros out of his head, he went directly to the tack room to collect the gear he needed to exercise one of the three horses he had to take out that afternoon.

Checking the gear over, he let the easy rhythm of the stables slide over him. The clip clop of hooves on concrete, the whinny of horses talking to each other over their stalls, the clink of metal on metal as an animal was shod filled him with a sense of peace he hadn't felt in months.

If he wasn't consumed with the thought of the hundreds of emails piling up in his inbox back in New York, the two massive deals his brother Joaquim, director of Salazar's European operations, was stickhandling for him, it would almost be idyllic.

"Hey Hollywood." Tommy, one of his fellow grooms, stuck his head in the tack room. "Boss's daughter wants to see you."

Uh-oh. He'd done such a good job of avoiding Cecily after that moment they'd shared in the stable. Was pretty sure she'd been avoiding him too. So why seek him out now?

He joined a group of grooms congregated in front of the tiny kitchen, Cecily holding court in their midst. Dressed in jeans and a sleeveless shirt that hugged her lithe curves, her hair caught up in a ponytail, she was a tiny, delectable package a man might want to eat for breakfast. Just not him, of course.

She turned to him once she'd finished her conversation

with the others. "I want to go for a hack up to the lake. I'd like you to come with me."

Oh, no. He recognized a bad idea when he heard one. "I still have three horses to exercise," he demurred smoothly. "Perhaps you can take someone else."

A female groom gaped at him. Tommy's brows rose. Cecily lifted her chin, training those vibrant blue eyes on him. "I would like *you* to come."

An order. Back to being mistress of all she surveyed, clearly.

He inclined his head. "Let me gather up a few things."

"Don't worry about food and water. I have that figured out."

He saddled up Jiango, a big, black stallion he'd had to exercise anyway. Tommy elbowed him as he walked the horse toward the yard. "Making an impression, Hollywood? A hundred bucks says you can't get past the ice cold exterior."

"Not looking to." He nipped that one in the bud. Rumors were the quickest way to blow his cover, particularly when they involved him and the boss's daughter.

Cecily eyed him as he brought Jiango to a halt in the yard. "I asked you along because I decided to take your advice and spend some downtime with Bacchus. I would have preferred to go by myself but my father won't let me ride up there alone. You will be the least talkative of the grooms."

So he was supposed to provide silent companionship to her highness? That he supposed he could do.

"Fair enough." He attempted to keep his eyes off her curvaceous rear as she turned, stuck her foot in the stirrup and climbed on Bacchus.

Usually, he went for tall, leggy women who matched him in physical attributes, but in Cecily's case, his mind immediately degenerated into all sorts of creative possibilities.

Bad Alejandro. He gave himself a mental slap and mounted Jiango. "How long a ride is it?"

"About an hour. It's gorgeous, you'll love it."

He did. Jiango, a powerful, Belgian-bred stallion, one of the Hargroves' up-and-coming young horses, more than kept up with Bacchus as they rode through pastures so green they looked frankly unreal, bounded by mile upon mile of picturesque white fence.

Aristocratic flowering trees with vibrant magenta and white blooms lined the track they rode on, providing shade to the long legged, elegant horses who dozed beneath a sky of the deepest blue.

The sun moved high in the sky as midday closed in. They left the pastures behind and entered a shady, light-dappled forest. Cecily turned to him, a mischievous glint in her eyes. "Want to show me what you've got, *Hollywood?*"

"If the prize is you not calling me that," he responded dryly, "I'm in."

"Done." A wider smile, a dazzling one that lit her face. "A race then, to the end of the road. First person over the creek wins." Her mouth pursed. "I will warn you—there are obstacles. You need to keep a sharp eye."

He'd gone cliff diving in Acapulco, bungee jumping in Thailand. He and the boys had even taken on sumo wrestlers in Japan. *This* would be a piece of cake.

"You're on," he said laconically. "You want a head start?"

Fire lit her gaze. She dug her heels into Bacchus and was flying down the road at breakneck speed before he'd even registered she'd moved. Kicking Jiango into a gallop, he gave him his head. Crouched low over the stallion's withers, he did his best to avoid the branches and obstacles that appeared out of nowhere, the odd one snagging him good.

Cecily held the lead. She was an insanely good rider, glued to the seat, but his horse had a longer stride than Bacchus's, helping him to make up ground. He was almost even with her when they neared what appeared to be the end of the road, the track growing steeper, plunging downhill to the creek. It took every bit of his experience to keep Jiango steady as they flew down the incline and headed for the water, the two horses even now.

He crouched forward in the saddle. Jiango jumped the water in a smooth, powerful movement. A gasp rang out behind him. Out of the corner of his eye, he saw Bacchus dig his feet in at the last moment, coming to a screeching halt on the rocks, nearly catapulting his rider over his head.

Somehow Cecily stayed in the saddle, regaining control as her horse skittered away from the water. He turned Jiango around and jumped back across the creek, bringing him to a halt beside Bacchus. Cheeks flushed, frustration glittering in her eyes, all the joy had gone out of Cecily's face.

"Guess that makes you the winner."

He frowned at the false bravado in her voice. "He normally jumps the creek?"

She nodded. "He loves it."

"Did your accident involve a water jump?"

"Yes, but he's jumped them since. His behavior isn't making any sense."

"Fear often doesn't make sense." He bunched his reins in one hand and sat back in the saddle. "A horse I worked with once had a bad crash on a really unusual fence that spooked him. He recovered, but the same thing happened to him that's happening to Bacchus. He wasn't just refusing on jumps that were new to him, he was refusing on jumps he had always been comfortable with—as if he didn't trust his rider anymore. Because, in his eyes, he'd led him astray."

"You think Bacchus believes I let him down?"

"I'm saying it's a possibility."

She chewed on her lip. "What did you do to make the horse right?"

"I gained his trust back."

"How?"

He lifted a brow. "You sure you want to learn from the 'school of psychobabble'?"

She gave him a reproachful look. "Yes."

He dismounted and walked over to Bacchus. "Get off," he instructed. "Take off your scarf."

"My scarf?"

"Yes—off."

She dismounted. Slid her fingers through the knot of her scarf and untied it, pulling it from her neck. Colt tied it around Bacchus's head, covering his eyes. The horse pawed the ground nervously, but stayed put.

"Take your shoes off and walk him across the stream."

She pulled off her riding boots and socks. Colt did the same. Boots in hand, he went first with Jiango. The water wasn't deep, but it moved fast. Jiango hesitated at the edge, but a firm tug on the reins had him moving forward.

Cecily and Bacchus followed. The moment Bacchus's hooves hit the running water, her horse jammed on the breaks and came to a grinding halt. Mouth set, Cecily walked back to him, stroked his neck and talked to him. By the time Alejandro and Jiango had reached the other side of the stream, Bacchus was cautiously making his way across.

"Take the blindfold off," he instructed when the pair walked up onto the bank.

Cecily removed the blindfold. Bacchus eyed the stream, sniffed the water, ears flickering as he registered he was on the other side.

"He knows he can trust you to get him to safety," Alejandro explained. "Now take him back across without the blindfold."

Horse and rider picked their way across the stream, then back again, Bacchus's confidence building with every step.

Cecily stopped Bacchus at his side. "What now?"

"We'll give him some time to think about it. See if he'll jump it on the way back."

She nodded. "It's just so strange. This is his favorite place."

"He's got something stuck in his head. Also," he added, eyes on hers, "he's absorbing your tension. I've been feeling it all week watching you ride. You've got to loosen up—change the dynamic between you two. Rebuild the trust."

She pushed her hair out of her face. "My coach doesn't believe in any of this. You're supposed to *make* the horse do what you want them to do."

"And that's working for you?"

Her eyes flashed. Lifting her chin, she nodded toward a path in the woods. "Lake's this way."

Cecily attempted to recapture her good mood as they walked the horses to her favorite picnic spot on the bank of the lake, but she was too agitated to manage it. For Bacchus to refuse a jump on his favorite ride was sucking what little hope she had left out of her that she would be ready to compete against the top riders in the world in just three weeks. It didn't seem possible.

She knew Colt was right, knew she needed to change the dynamic between her and Bacchus—she just didn't know how.

The sun at its midday peak, hot as the devil as her Grandmama Harper used to say, they tethered the horses in a shady spot under a tree. A mile wide, the lake was a stunning dark navy blue, bounded by forests of the deepest green. Quiet—eerily quiet except for the odd call of a bird or the splash of some water creature, it made her suddenly, inordinately aware of how very alone she and Colt were.

Perhaps this hadn't been such a good idea.

She retrieved the picnic lunch she'd had a farm hand drop off earlier while Colt spread the blanket out on a flat stretch of grass. He sprawled on top of it, taking the containers she handed him, a visual feast for the eye in his threadbare jeans and navy T-shirt.

Her thoughts immediately ventured into X-rated territory. She attempted to wrestle them back as she sorted out the lunch, but it proved almost impossible. He was a gorgeous male in the prime of his life, all coiled muscle and tensile strength, the effect he had on her core deep.

Heart ticking faster, every inch of her skin utterly and irrefutably aware of him, she sat down on the blanket and served up the lunch of fried chicken and potato salad the cook had provided.

Colt demolished it with a cold beer. Her appetite seemingly not in attendance, whether because of her misery or her intense awareness of the man beside her, she pushed her plate away and nursed the wine cooler she'd brought for herself, eyes on the water.

Colt rolled up a towel from the basket and propped it behind his head, stretching out with feline grace in the baking sun. She noted the careful distance he kept between them, the wary glint in his eyes whenever he looked at her. And suddenly, felt like a fool.

"I'm sorry I strong-armed you into coming up here with me."

He paused, beer bottle halfway to his lips. "I'm enjoying it. You were right—it's amazing up here. I was surprised, though, you didn't want to bring a friend."

"I don't have any." She gave a self-conscious shrug.

"At least no real ones. My best friend, Melly, decided we weren't friends anymore after I won the junior championship. I'm on the road so much, there's really been no opportunity to make any new friends other than the people I compete with and those relationships only go so deep."

"That must get lonely."

"I'm better off with companionship of the four legged variety. Horses are endlessly loyal and they don't talk back to me."

His mouth quirked. "They also can't provide anything in the way of strength and solidarity."

She tipped her head to the side, curious. "Is that what your friends mean to you?"

"A big part of it, yes. We go back to college, my best friends and I. We've been through some pretty amazing times together—both good and bad. There's a bond there that's unbreakable even with the distance between us. One of us needs something—the rest of us jump."

A pang went through her. She wished she had that. Someone who knew you so well you could just be yourself rather than what everyone else thought you should be. But she'd never been good at fostering those types of relationships.

"That would be nice," she said quietly, "to have friends like that."

He studied her for a long moment. "So Melly turned out to be a dud. Find someone else who deserves your friendship. You can't spend every waking minute riding a horse."

"According to my coach that's exactly what I should be doing."

"No," he disagreed. "You shouldn't. Success in life comes from opening yourself up to new horizons. *Balance*." He lifted a brow. "What about boyfriends? You must have them."

"Too busy."

"Surely men pursue you?"

She took a sip of her drink. Cradled the bottle between her hands. "My parents want me to marry Knox Henderson. He owns half of Texas. They keep throwing us together, but I have no interest."

"Why?" An amused glitter filled his gaze. "Is he unattractive? Too old? Too boring?"

"He's young, attractive and rich. And he knows it."

"What's not to like about that? A woman needs a strong, successful man."

She rolled her eyes.

"Did you even give him a chance?"

"Define 'give him a chance'."

"Did you kiss him?"

"Yes. No spark." She gave him a considering glance, having overheard Tommy's earlier remark. "I know the bet the boys in the barn have going."

"What bet?"

She waved a hand at him. "You don't have to play dumb. They think I'm a cold fish. And maybe I am."

He rubbed a palm over his jaw. Eyed her. "Was this Knox even a good kisser?"

"I'm sure many women would say yes. Not me. He's coming to the barn party on Friday night. You'll get to meet him then."

"About that," he murmured. "It's very nice of you to invite the staff but I have nothing to wear. I actually *am* Cinderella."

"You get paid today. Buy something in town." Somehow the comparison of Colt and Knox in the same room was far too intriguing to resist.

"It was my mama's idea to include the staff," she told him. "She always loved the family atmosphere it created. Kay, my stepmother, wanted to cut the tradition out when she came here. A needless expense, she said." Her mouth twisted as she brushed a stray hair out of her face. "I ve-toed it. It set the tone for our tempestuous relationship."

"It's a very nice tradition." Colt took a sip of his beer. "You must miss your mother. You lost her very young."

Her smile faded. "Every day." She looked down at the bottle in her hand. "She died up here. That's why Daddy doesn't like me coming alone."

He sat up on his elbows. "I assumed she died while she was competing."

She shook her head. "She and Daddy had an argument. I know, because the whole house heard it. It was a bad one—worse than usual. Daddy flew off to New York on business, Mama left the house in a state and came up here without telling anyone. When I finished my lessons with my tutor I went looking for her. I knew she'd be up here because it was her favorite place.

"I found her hat on the ground. I knew something was wrong. We searched for hours but we couldn't find her. We were on our way back to the house when we found Zeus, her horse. Mama had gotten thrown from him and he was dragging her by the stirrup." She pressed her lips together, a throb pulsing her insides. "He was taking her home."

"I'm sorry," Colt said quietly. "That must have been awful."

The worst day of her life. Her heart squeezed. What she wouldn't do to have her wise, kind mother here now to help her sort out the mess she was in.

She studied the play of the sunlight on the water, a dancing, rippling pattern that continually changed form. "I don't think my father's ever forgiven himself for it. I'm not sure *I've* forgiven him for it. I mean I know rationally, it wasn't his fault, but I miss her so much."

"Did you ever find out what they were arguing about?"

She shook her head. "Daddy won't talk about it. One of the maids told me she heard them arguing about Zeus, but that doesn't make any sense. Daddy never interfered in Mama's horse stuff."

He took a swig of his beer. "Isn't the rumor Zeus was sired by Diablo?"

She laughed. "Oh, that's not true. Everyone likes to make up these crazy stories about him. Demeter, Zeus' mama, was bred with a French stallion named Nightshade—an equally impressive match. Nightshade was a three-time European champion, that's where Bacchus gets his jumping ability from."

He inclined his head. "Funny how rumors get started."

She watched a loon sail elegantly across the glass-like surface of the water, its haunting cry echoing the dull throb inside of her. Being here it always hurt ten times worse, her emotions already far too close to the surface.

"She wasn't just my mother," she said quietly, heat gathering at the back of her eyes. "She was my best friend. My coach, my confidante, my *hero*. She taught me to ride before I could walk, took me to all the shows with her. We were inseparable. I wanted to *be* her when I grew up."

A silence fell between them. "And you want to win for her," Colt said finally.

She nodded, the tears stinging the backs of her eyes threatening to spill over. "I want to do what she didn't have time to do."

Suddenly all the pieces of the puzzle that was Cecily Hargrove were falling into place. Alejandro studied her over the rim of his beer bottle, heart squeezing despite his attempts to remain unmoved. How could he?

He'd watched her kill herself over the past week, wondering what ghosts drove her. Now he knew. But beating herself and Bacchus into the ground over and over again until there was nothing left of either of them wasn't going to fix the problem—wasn't going to fix *them*.

He'd seen glimpses of the real Cecily on the way up here today. Her spirit. Her joy. What she must have been like as a competitor when her demons weren't chasing her. Watching her now was like watching light turn into dark.

Setting his beer bottle down, he turned to face her. "You know what I think," he said softly, studying those beautiful, haunted eyes. "I think you don't know who you are anymore. Who you're riding for. I think you're riding for everyone *but* yourself."

She frowned. "The accident—"

"Was just the tip of the iceberg." He tapped his head. "When *this* gets messed up—when what you want, what everyone else wants, when too much damn pressure starts to build—*no one* can perform."

Her eyes widened. "Bacchus is a problem."

"Yes," he agreed, "he is. But *you* are the bigger problem. Until you figure *you* out, until you decide who you're doing this for, you have no hope of making that team. You might as well pack it up and throw in the towel right now."

Her gaze dropped away from his. She was silent for so long he realized he had gone too far. "I'm sorry," he murmured. "I shouldn't have—"

"No," she said, lifting her head, eyes glazed with unshed tears. "You're right. I have no idea who I am anymore. I've spent my whole life doing what everyone else expects of me. Giving up a normal life—leaving school, traveling eight months of the year every year so I can make this team..." She sank her teeth into her bottom lip. "What if I don't? It's all I know—it's my entire *identity*."

His throat tightened. "Then you find something else to be. But I don't think that's going to happen, Cecily. You clearly have the talent. Now you need to find the *reason*."

A tear slid down her cheek. Then another. A curse left his lips. He pulled her into his arms, his chin coming down on top of her silky hair, her petite body curved against his.

"You need to take control," he murmured. "Decide what you want. This has to be you, Cecily, no one else."

She cried against his chest. He held her, stroking his hand over her hair. How could he do anything else when she had no one, literally no one, to confide in?

He murmured comforting words against her silky cheek. Discovered her hair smelled like lemons and sunshine—that she was far more intoxicating than he'd ever imagined she would be, curled so tightly in his arms.

She finally pulled back, tears slowing. "Thank you," she said. "No one is ever honest with me. Everyone tells me what I want to hear rather than what I need to hear. Except my parents. They just give me orders."

He tucked a chunk of her hair behind her ear. Ran his thumbs across her cheeks to brush the tears away. "Then maybe you need to change that too. You're old enough to own your own decisions—your own successes and failures."

She nodded, eyes on his. Her lashes lowered, sweeping across her cheeks as the temperature between them changed and suddenly everything was focused on the fact that she was in his lap, her arms wrapped around him and really he should be disentangling himself *right now*.

"Colt?"

Distracted, he brought his gaze back up to hers. The reminder he wasn't who he'd said he was, that this *couldn't happen*, should have been enough to have him ending it right now, but the hesitant look in her blue eyes commanded him instead.

"That night in the barn—was I imagining that you wanted to kiss me?"

Por amor a Deus. How was he supposed to answer that? Lie and he would hurt her, something he wasn't willing to do. But telling her the truth wasn't an option either.

"I don't think I should answer that question."

"Why?"

"Because I work for you. Because it isn't appropriate."

"This is already past appropriate," she murmured, eyes on his mouth. "And you've already answered my question by not answering."

"Then we should consider the subject closed." He reached up to disentangle her arms from around his neck. She kept them where they were.

"I think I should test my theory out."

"What theory?"

"That you will be a better kisser than Knox."

Oh, no. He shook his head. "I think we should leave the answer to the theoretical realm."

"I don't." She curved her fingers around the back of his neck and drew his mouth down to hers. He should have stopped it right there, should have exercised the sanity he should have had, but he wasn't going to reject her—not in her ultra-vulnerable state. And, if the truth be known, he wanted to kiss her. *Badly.* Had since that night in the barn.

Lush and full, not quite practiced, the brush of her lips against his sent a sizzle over every inch of his skin. *This was such a bad idea.*

He relaxed beneath her touch, allowed her to play. He'd give it a minute, make it good and get out of Dodge.

"You have an amazing mouth," Cecily breathed against his lips. "But you aren't kissing me back."

"Self-preservation," he murmured before he splayed his fingers around her delicate jaw, angled her mouth the way he wanted it and took control.

Her sweet, heady taste exploded across his senses. As good as he'd imagined it to be—maybe better. Fingers stroking over the silky skin of her cheek, he explored the voluptuous line of her mouth with his own, acquainting himself with every plump, perfect centimeter.

When skin against skin didn't seem to be enough, he

brought his teeth and tongue into play, nipping, stroking, lathing. A gasp escaped her lips. He took advantage of the opportunity and closed his mouth over hers, taking the kiss deeper, mating his tongue with hers. Twining her fingers into the hair at his nape, she followed his lead, sliding her tongue against his, turning the kiss into an intimate, seductive exploration that fried his brain.

Santo Deus, but she was responsive, the taste of them together perfection. He fought the desire to explore the rest of her curvy, hot body with his mouth and tongue. To discover how sweet she really was.

In his world, kisses like this led to hot, explosive sex. In *this* world, however, it absolutely, positively could not happen.

His rational brain kicked in. He broke the kiss, sank his fingers into her waist and lifted her off him and placed her back on the blanket.

Cheeks flushed, eyes on his, Cecily pushed a hand through her hair. "That was—"

"Proof you aren't a cold fish," he said, pushing to his feet. "Now we forget it happened."

She eyed him. "Colt—"

He shook his head. "You know my MO. Here today, gone tomorrow. You don't want to get involved with me, Cecily. Trust me."

CHAPTER THREE

FORGET IT HAPPENED? Cecily couldn't do anything *but* think about that kiss with Colt in the days leading up to the Hargroves' annual summer party. It infiltrated her thoughts, her dreams, her practice sessions, rendering her concentration less than ideal.

To know that kind of passion existed, the explosive kind she'd felt with Colt, had turned her world upside down. Not even with Davis, as crazy as she'd been about him, had she experienced that kind of chemistry. And yet rationality told her Colt was right—the best thing for them to do was ignore it. She had to focus on making this team and Colt would move on again soon.

She put her focus, instead, on her new approach to fixing her and Bacchus's relationship. On fixing *her*. She was twenty-five years old. It *was* time for her to take charge of her life and career. If she didn't start directing things, figuring out who she was and what she wanted, everyone else was going to do it for her. And that was unacceptable.

With Dale's coaching getting her and Bacchus nowhere fast, she began working with Colt in the afternoons, exploring some of the techniques he'd used on his case similar to Bacchus's. Given her horse had, in fact, jumped the creek on the way home from the lake, she thought there might be something there.

They were making baby steps—tiny amounts of progress. Now if only she could make herself immune to the man giving the instructions.

Kay caught her as she walked into the house to get ready for the party, insisting she come greet the Hendersons who would stay the weekend. Toeing off her muddy boots in the entrance way, she walked into the salon. Knox was as flirtatious as ever—she as uninterested as ever. Exercising the briefest of social niceties, she excused herself to go to her room.

Her father intercepted her before she could, pulling her into his study. "Dale tells me you're still working with Colt Banyon," he said, shutting the door. "Why?'

She lifted her chin. "Because I want to. Because I think it's going to help Bacchus."

Clayton Hargrove leaned back against his desk, tall, cool, southern elegance in gray trousers and a white shirt. "What you're doing is wasting your time. That stuff is nonsense he's teaching you."

"I'm going to decide what's right and wrong for me from now on."

"Excuse me?"

She crossed her arms over her chest. "I am twenty-five years old, Daddy. I'm not a child. I need to start managing my own life and career."

Her father scowled. "Colt Banyon is a drifter. He wanders from stable to stable. You don't know anything about him or his credentials."

"I know I trust him. And he comes with impeccable credentials. Cliff wouldn't hire anyone with anything less."

"I could fire him."

A surge of fury rose up inside her. "You fire him and I'll withdraw from the Geneva event."

"You wouldn't do that."

"Try me."

"Dammit, Cecily," her father bellowed. "See some sense here."

"I am seeing some. Finally." She bit the inside of her mouth, deciding to go for broke now that she was knee deep. "What were you and Mama arguing about the day she died?"

Her father frowned. "What does that have to do with this?"

"Nothing. I just want to know."

A stony expression consumed his face. "Nothing that concerns you. It was a private matter between your mother and I."

"After which she broke the cardinal rule and went riding by herself?" Her lips set in a tight line. "She knew better than that, Daddy. Isabella said she looked knocked sideways after you left. What happened between you two?"

He shook his head. "It's ancient history. Let it go."

"I've tried. It hasn't worked." She fixed her gaze on his. "You pretend you don't miss her, but you do. You pretend it never happened, but it did." She pushed a stray hair out of her face with a trembling hand. "I'll never stop wondering what happened that day. What made her do something so stupid. And I'll never stop missing her. Because, apparently, I'm the only one in this family who has a heart."

Spinning on her heel, she stalked to the door.

"Cecily."

She wrenched the door open, walked through it and slammed it shut. Kay and the Hendersons gave her a bemused look as she stalked through the salon and headed for her room. She ignored them all.

"You ready to go?"

Colt opened the door to his cabin to find Tommy, decked out in a checked shirt and jeans, lounging against the doorframe, a pink Kentucky sunset staining the sky behind him.

He shook his head. "I was thinking I might skip it."

Tommy waved his hat at him. "You can't skip it. It's the social event of the season. All you can drink beer and beautiful women… What's not to like?"

The fact that one gorgeous woman in particular was

finding her way beneath his skin—a woman he couldn't have. That he was a day away from completing this challenge of Sebastien's. He wasn't about to blow it now.

Antonio's phone call this morning appealing for a stay on his private island as the paparazzi chased his family for photos amidst a scandal cemented the need to get out of here unscathed. He'd given the Italian the green light to spend his honeymoon on the island and counted his lucky stars it wasn't him.

He rolled his shoulders. "I pulled a muscle carrying that beam today. Think I'll hole up here and read a book."

"Oh, come on, Hollywood." Tommy flashed him a yellow-toothed grin. "You're tougher than that. Get your boots on and let's go. We'll find you a gorgeous woman to work that shoulder of yours out."

Deciding resistance was futile, Alejandro pulled on the new blue shirt and jeans he'd bought in town, applied some aftershave and tugged on his boots.

The party was in full swing when they arrived at one of the bigger thoroughbred barns that wasn't in use. The cavernous space had been done up for the occasion with fairy lights strung from the vaulted ceiling, a bar in one corner and a well-known country band playing in another. High cruiser tables scattered about the space offered the hundreds of guests a lounging spot to enjoy the food and drink being circulated as they enjoyed a lazy, exceedingly warm Kentucky night.

True to Tommy's promise, there were dozens of beautiful women in attendance, clad in pretty summer dresses. Alejandro had always appreciated a southern woman's charms—the big hair, the ultra-feminine way they dressed, the soft, seductive voices—he found it sexy as hell. But tonight only one of those women caught his eye and it was the one who could flay a man's skin with her razor sharp tongue one minute, then slay him with a husky, vulnerable drawl the next.

Cecily wore a burnt orange dress that seemed to have been painted on, its short skirt ending at mid-thigh, exposing smooth, toned legs he couldn't take his eyes off. When he finally managed to, a plunging V-neckline revealed more delectable curves. It took very little of his imagination to imagine what the rest of her would look like without clothes. *Utterly sensational.*

He pulled his gaze away from temptation and up to her face. Unfortunately, there was more of it there. Her hair set in big, loose curls, a smoky eye makeup and vivid red lip color making her look less angelic tonight and more irresistible siren, she was jaw-droppingly beautiful.

She turned her head, as if sensing his perusal. A charge vibrated the air between them, sizzling his blood in his veins in a hot, restless purr. He sucked in a breath, the need to have, to *possess* something that was off limits to him an experience he was unused to having.

He wanted her. Up against a wall would be nice, those fabulous legs wrapped around his waist, his mouth buried in her silky hair while he gave her everything he had. But, really, he was fairly certain any position would do.

"Pretty boy's back," Tommy murmured. "Wonder when he's finally going to get the message she isn't interested."

Alejandro didn't respond. He was too busy sizing up the tall, muscular male at Cecily's side. His dark blond hair slicked back from his handsome face, an air of supreme confidence surrounding him, Knox Henderson wore the look of a man who knew what he wanted: the woman standing beside him in a very sexy red dress whose smile was not at all right.

Not my problem, he told himself. *You can't have her.* He'd been telling himself that all week.

He should have stayed away tonight just like he'd planned. Should have listened to his instincts.

Cecily swallowed hard as she stared at Colt. Knox could have told her one of his oil wells was spouting twenty-four-carat gold and it still wouldn't have penetrated her brain. Her skin shimmered with an awareness that seemed layers deep, her pulse ratcheted up a notch and her breath lodged in her throat as she took in the man she'd told herself she hadn't been waiting for.

Dressed in a pair of dark jeans and a light blue shirt rolled up at the sleeves, the color a perfect foil for his dark, dreamy good looks, Colt was God's gift to women and that was all. But it was the unguarded look on his face that had her complete attention.

Open and direct, *hot*, he'd forgotten to assume that mask he always wore. The horse was most definitely out of the barn and it sent a shiver up her spine.

"We should dance," Knox murmured in her ear. "I haven't managed one with you yet."

Because she didn't want to lead him on. Because he'd already knocked back a couple of stiff bourbons and Knox got handsy when he drank. Because the only person she wanted to dance with was Colt.

Knox, however, was already setting his empty glass on a cruiser table and pulling her onto the dance floor. To compound her problem, the band launched into a slow tune, allowing him to pull her close.

"Why do you play hard to get?" he murmured. "Come on Cecily, give me a break. What do I have to do?"

She tipped her head back to look up at him. "I am hard to get. I've told you more than once, I can't see us together, Knox. It just isn't there."

"Why not?"

"It isn't the kind of thing I can explain. It just is or isn't."

"You won't even try." His hand dropped lower on her hip, dangerously close to her bottom. "You wear a dress like this, what am I supposed to do? Name your price, sugar. You want a stable full of the best horses in the world? They're yours. A place in the south of France? I'll give it to you. Some extra money for upkeep? It'll be in your bank account."

She eyed him. "Upkeep?"

"Well you know, most women I know like to do a nip or a tuck here or there. Keep up appearances." He shrugged. "I'm good with that. It's like tuning up a car every once in a while. I'd consider it part of the maintenance budget."

Her jaw dropped. "I'm twenty-five, Knox. What kind of maintenance do you think I need?"

"I didn't say you *needed* it. I said the option was there if you wanted it."

Lord have mercy. This was going to get ugly if she didn't keep her mouth shut. Chin lifting at a defiant angle, she eyed his handsome, superior face. "The fact is…I'm interested in someone else."

A glimmer entered his blue gaze. "Who?"

"It doesn't matter."

"Sure it does. I am more than a bit curious to see who's penetrated that frigid exterior of yours. I was starting to think it an impossible feat."

Her insides contracted at the direct hit. It was her Achilles' heel that no one would ever want her for who she truly was. Her biggest fear that she would only ever be valuable for the legacy she carried. Davis had made sure of that.

She gave him an unflinching look. "Quit acting ugly, Knox. Bow out gracefully."

His mouth twisted. "*You* could have bowed out gracefully. I flew hundreds of miles to see you, Cecily. I blew off a client to be here. You could have at least given me a heads-up."

Damn Kay and her meddling. A tense silence fell between them as the song dragged on. The near bullet she'd dodged became vividly clear. As Knox's wife she would have been a high-priced possession, bought for her looks and poise. Another ornament to add to his mantelpiece. He would never have *understood* her like Colt did.

She searched for him in the crowd. Found him in a group of stable hands who were fraternizing with some of the locals. Sharp knives of jealousy lanced through her as a beautiful brunette who lived in town pulled him onto the dance floor.

Slim with stunning green eyes, her mother would have called her a tall drink of water. The brunette said something to Colt that made him laugh as he drew her into his arms, a lazy, sexy laugh she'd never heard him utter before.

Her skin stung. The old Cecily would have pretended she didn't care. Would have continued to deny how she felt—closed herself off behind her walls. The new Cecily found she couldn't.

Alejandro threw back a long, cool beer after a few sets on the dance floor, the brunette glued to his side. She was stunning, absolutely his type, but he abhorred meaningless chatter, the only kind, it seemed, she knew.

A scan of the space determined Cecily was still missing. Had been for the better part of a half-hour. Her smile, the not quite right one he'd been trying to ignore, flashed through his head.

"Will you excuse me?" he drawled to the brunette, setting his bottle down on a table. "I need some fresh air."

Winding his way through the crowd before she could invite herself along, which he was sure she would, he exited the barn. It was deserted outside, the faint sound of music and chatter spilling out into a sultry, warm Kentucky night.

He almost missed Cecily. He caught her on his second scan, arms folded over the top of the fence, face lifted to a star-blanketed sky. His steps soundless, he joined her, slinging his elbows over the fence.

She turned a storm-tossed gaze on him. "Leave your fan club inside?"

He ignored the jibe. "You going to tell me what's wrong?"

She sighed. Pushed a hand through her hair. "I had a fight with Daddy. A good one. Then Knox and I tangled just now."

"About?"

"I told him it's never happening between us." Her mouth tightened. "He's not good with taking no for an answer."

"In what way?"

"He was angry. He wasn't very nice about it."

"Let him be angry. You made your decision."

"I know. It's just our families are good friends. And—" she bit her lip.

"What?"

"He called me frigid."

His fingers curled tight around the rail. Now he wanted to kick the guy's teeth in. Damn good thing it was a sure-fire way to get his cover blown or he would.

"He's frustrated," he rasped. "Forget about him. What were you arguing with your father about?"

"You." She turned to face him. "Daddy doesn't want me working with you and Bacchus. I told him too bad, I'm taking charge of my life and career now."

Cristo. Shining a light on himself was not what he'd had in mind when he'd agreed to help her with her horse.

"You might consider taking baby steps," he counseled. "Give yourself time to think. Blowing your whole life up right now isn't a good idea with everything you have on your plate."

Her lashes lowered. "I just feel like I've wasted enough time."

He shook his head. "You are so young, Cecily. You have your whole life ahead of you."

The band began to play a new song, the notes wafting along the breeze that rustled the leaves of the aristocratic magnolia tree above. It was their most notable tune—the lead singer's raspy, deep voice crooning out the plaintive notes of the angsty ballad.

"I love this song," Cecily said quietly. "It's about a girl who only ever gets what she doesn't want. How it's her curse to walk through this world alone." She pressed a fist to her chest. "It gets me right here."

His heart stuttered. She didn't have to explain why the song affected her so much. It was *her*.

He held out his hand. "Dance with me then."

Her beautiful blue eyes fixed on his. Stepping away from the fence, she laced her fingers through his, slid her other hand around his waist and moved into his arms. It was a mistake, he knew it, as he pulled her close. But her damn vulnerability got to him every time.

They danced in the moonlight, in perfect sync, silent as they enjoyed the song. Even the cynic in Alejandro knew it for the rarity it was—to be so in tune with someone, talking was unnecessary.

She drifted closer, eliminating the respectable distance he'd forged between them. Her perfectly proportioned curves brushed the length of his body, her silky hair caressed his jaw, her breath teased the bare skin at the open neck of his shirt—heating his blood in all the most dangerous ways.

"Cecily..." he murmured.

"This isn't working."

"What isn't?"

"Trying to ignore this thing between us."

His jaw set. "It's the right thing to do."

"Why?" Challenging. *Provocative.*

"I've already explained that."

"You want me," she said pointedly. "I saw it on your face tonight when you walked in. That kiss we shared was amazing, you know it was."

"And that's as far as it goes."

She stepped even closer, lifting up on tip toe to bring her mouth to his ear. "I can't concentrate. All I can think about is that kiss. *You.* The entire time I was dancing with Knox I was thinking about you."

Blood pounded his temples. He was about to shut it down, to tell her no more kisses were happening when a smooth drawl drifted across the air.

"So this is where you're getting it from." Knox Henderson stepped out of the shadows, a puff of round smoke from his cigar rising up in the air. He set his gaze on Cecily. "If I'd known you like to get down and dirty with a stable hand I would have lost the suits along with the kid gloves."

A cold fire flared in Alejandro's gut. He set Cecily away from him, stepped forward and faced the man casually puffing away on the cigar. The glazed look in Henderson's eyes said he'd had more than a few drinks.

"I think you need to take that back," Alejandro said quietly, "and go back inside."

"Oh, but I'm curious," the other man demurred. "She leads me on, lets me fly down here, only for me to find she's screwing someone else. Can't blame me for wanting to check out the competition."

Alejandro took a step closer, fingers curling into fists at his sides. "Now you have. Accept that she isn't interested and step inside."

Henderson lifted a brow. "Accept she wants to bang

a stable hand? Sorry if I can't stomach that. It's just too much."

Alejandro moved so quickly, Henderson was still drawing a puff of his cigar when he wrapped a fist around his shirt collar. "I'm giving you one more chance," he snarled. "Apologize."

The other man's mouth curved in a mean smile. "I don't think so."

A fist connected with Alejandro's jaw in a lightning fast punch Alejandro never saw coming. A white-hot sting radiating through his head, he swung his fist in an upper right hook. A fractured cry escaping her throat, Cecily jumped between them, Alejandro barely managing to pull his fist back before it connected with her instead of Henderson.

"Stop it. Both of you. *Stop."*

Fury consuming him, Alejandro was almost past the point of listening. Only the panicked look on Cecily's face pulled him back from the edge.

Cecily glared at Knox. "Inside," she ordered, pointing toward the barn. *"Right now."*

Knox looked down at her, a derisive smile curling his lips. "You know what? You're right. You aren't worth it."

Cecily escorted Knox back to the party, not trusting him not to instigate something else if she didn't. Seeing him safely to a group of friends, she took some ice from one of the coolers in the serving area and left via the back entrance.

Taking a circuitous route to the staff accommodations so no one would see her, she knocked on the door to Colt's cabin. He opened the door a moment later. Her gaze flew to the red mark on his jaw, some swelling already visible in the moonlight.

"Oh, God, Colt, I am so sorry."

He put a hand to his jaw. "It's fine. No big deal."

"It's swelling already." She held up the bag of ice. "We can put this on it."

"I can," he corrected, reaching for the bag.

She held it behind her back. "Let me come in and do it. I feel so guilty. I can't believe Knox was such a buffoon."

He fixed a dark, unyielding stare on her. "Give me the ice, Cecily. You know you coming in is a bad idea."

She firmed her mouth. "Let me come in and make sure you're okay, then I'll leave."

They stared each other down. "Fine," he said, stepping back.

She slipped through the door and kicked off her shoes. Extremely basic, the cabin consisted of a queen-sized bed, a chest of drawers, an armchair by the window and a tiny cooking area. Colt hadn't personalized the space, in keeping with his drifter persona.

When that struck a raw place in her throat, she shoved it from her head and moved to the kitchen area to wrap the ice in a towel.

"Sit," she said, pointing to the chair.

He did. She perched on the arm and pressed the cloth full of ice to his jaw, making him wince.

"He hurt you."

He gave her a grim look. "You might have let me retaliate."

"It would have cost you your job." Knox would have made sure of it.

A silence fell between them in the intimate stillness of the cabin. "I asked Daddy about Mama today," she finally said to break it. "About what they were arguing about the day she died."

"What did he say?"

"He wouldn't tell me. He said it was between him and my mother. That I should let it go."

"Maybe you should." He eyed her. "Marriages get rocky. Trust me. It's a fact of life."

"Was your parents' marriage difficult?"

"My parents don't actually *have* a marriage." Cynicism stained his voice. "They have an open-ended partnership they draw upon when needed—utterly dysfunctional and scarily efficient all at the same time."

"Oh." Maybe that explained some of the closed-offness of him. Why he never settled down. "I'm sorry."

"Don't be. I'm sure it works better than a great percentage of American marriages."

She had no doubt it did. Except she knew the magic did exist, because, despite the fiery nature of their union, her parents had loved each other. *Adored* each other. She just hadn't found that magic yet.

A dark hollow dug its way through her insides, Knox's words ringing in her ears. Maybe it was true. Maybe she wasn't capable of love—of giving herself to someone else. Maybe she would never have it.

She adjusted the ice higher on his jaw. "I know I should let it go—what happened that day—it's just Mama's behavior was so off. Something never felt right about it. I think maybe if I understood what happened I could let go."

"And maybe it would only confuse you more."

"Maybe."

His sexy scent wrapped itself around her. No point in wearing that in the barn, she conceded, but she couldn't help but absorb how perfectly the spicy, masculine scent highlighted this more urbane version of Colt. How utterly incapable she was of ignoring either version of him—the sweaty, earthy male she encountered in the barn every day or this drop dead gorgeous version of him. Both were irresistible.

And suddenly she didn't want to ignore it. Suddenly, she didn't care about what was wise or smart anymore, about maintaining concentration on the end goal. Perhaps it was Knox's cruel words or Davis's humiliation of her that drove her—but she needed to know that kiss with Colt hadn't just been a flash in the pan. That she was *worth* something. That Knox was wrong.

"Colt?"

"Mm?" She could see the dark glitter of attraction staining his amazing eyes. *That* he couldn't hide.

"Let me stay."

"No." Hard. Implacable.

She bit her lip. Swallowed her pride, because sometimes it got in the way of expressing what her heart truly wanted—this inability of hers to be vulnerable.

She set her gaze on his. "I'm not good at this—you know I'm not. I'm an expert at pushing people away, at avoiding intimate relationships. Maybe it's because I've been hurt too much. Maybe I'm simply not *capable* of it. But with you," she said solemnly, "with the chemistry we share, it's innate, it's just there. And I need that tonight. I need to be with you."

An emotion she couldn't read flickered in his eyes. "Cecily—"

She held up a hand. "What I'm saying is I want this one night. I know you're going to walk away—it's good that you are, because my career is the most important thing in the world to me right now. But this, *us*, I want to know it."

CHAPTER FOUR

ALEJANDRO'S HEART JOLTED in his chest. He could have taken just about anything she'd thrown at him and put the breaks on this insanity—but *that*—that was like a kick to the teeth.

He ran a hand over his jaw, unfamiliar wiry stubble scraping his palm. How could he say yes? *How could he say no?* What must it have cost her to expose herself like that? And yet she had.

Reason battled with madness. So he gave her that one night she was asking for? Showed to her, *proved* to her for one night of her life that she was special, that she was worth more than that jerk Knox Henderson. That she should hold out for everything she wanted and deserved. Was that really so crazy?

And really, how much worse could this get? He'd already gotten so involved, made such a mess of it, that nothing short of him walking away from here in a day's time was going to fix it.

He raked a hand through his hair. "I'm not sure your head is on straight right now. That you're not going to wake up tomorrow with a massive 'seize the moment' hangover and regret this."

She shook her head. "I know what I'm doing."

Alejandro considered himself an honorable man. A good man. But as Cecily slipped off the chair and moved her fingers to the side zipper of her dress, he knew he wasn't a saint.

Eyes on his, she slipped the sexy red dress off her shoulders and let it slip to the floor. His throat went dry. The lacy underwear she wore beneath it was a rich garnet that contrasted deliciously with her honey gold skin, the body the lace encased so perfectly formed it surpassed every one of his earlier fantasies.

"You should lock the door," he rasped.

Her eyes glittered. She kicked the dress aside, walked to the door and locked it. As she turned and moved back to him, her stride smooth and unashamed in her nakedness, a switch flicked inside of him and he was completely and irrevocably lost.

He pulled her onto his lap, her legs straddling his thighs. Cupping her nape, he exerted a light pressure to bring her mouth down to his. Open mouthed and hot, their kisses inflamed his senses. His hands at her hips, he held her in place for his delectation, each kiss unlike any he'd experienced before—so pure and real they stripped him bare. As if they were uncovering layers of each other that had yet to be explored.

Wanting, *needing* to touch her beautiful body, he ran his palms up the hot, smooth skin of her back, luxuriating in her silken perfection. A sigh slipped from her lips, a decadent, hedonistic release of air that made him smile.

"You like my callused hands?"

She pushed back to look at him. "I have this fantasy…"

His blood heated. "Which is?"

A self-conscious shimmer invaded her brilliant blue gaze. "The night we were in the stables…when you were giving Bacchus that massage." Her silky long lashes shaded her cheeks. "I was imagining your hands on me. How they would feel…what you would *do* with them."

The warmth in his blood deepened to full-fired lust. He lifted a brow. "You want my hands on you, *querida?* It would be my pleasure. *If* you promise to submit to a fantasy of mine."

Her eyes widened. "Which is?"

"You'll find out in a few minutes," he murmured, scooping her off the chair and heading for the bed.

"Spanish," she murmured as he set her down. "Is that your heritage?"

Damn, he hadn't even registered the slip. "Yes," he lied, thankful the word was the same in Portuguese and Spanish. *He might well go to hell for this.* He truly might. But his intentions were good.

Cecily watched him as he stripped off his shirt, eyes darkening to a deep slate blue. "You have an amazing body."

He threw the shirt on the floor, his fingers moving to the button of his jeans. "Strip shows are on your list of fantasies?"

Her mouth curved. "If it's you, yes."

He slipped the zipper down, her admission turning him hard as stone. Stuck his fingers in the sides of his jeans and dispensed with them in one quick movement. Kicking the denim aside, he straightened to find her eyes glued to his close-fitting white briefs. More than a bit aroused by the whole show, by the thought of having her, his erection was thick, straining against the fabric.

"I might switch fantasies," she murmured.

"Oh, but that's not how this game is played," he drawled. "Lie down and roll over."

A flush touched her cheeks. Then she obeyed. He drank her in, testosterone sizzling every nerve ending. She had the most amazing backside he'd ever seen. Firm and curvaceous, toned by hours in the saddle, it was the best part of her by far.

He swallowed past the lust clogging his throat. He intended to show that part of her anatomy his deepest idolatry.

He knelt on the bed beside her. Placed a palm on the small of her back and settled her as he would a nervous filly. A shiver moved through her. Tracing his palm up over her back, then down over her bottom and legs, he absorbed every dip and curve of her beautiful body.

Need gnawed at the edges of his self-control, goading him on. He straddled her. Set his mouth to the back of her neck and took a long, deep taste of her. She arched beneath him, a low moan leaving her throat. "That's not hands."

He ran his tongue along the curve of her shoulder. "I made no promise about the exclusive use of hands."

Not a word in response.

Down her body he went, his touch reverential as he explored every inch of her, kneading her silken flesh. Her whimpers, the way she came alive beneath his hands, fired his hunger. His erection thickening, growing with every low moan, he leashed himself with superhuman effort.

Finally, he reached her amazing backside. The silk thong barely covered the twin smooth globes. Cupping her in his hands, he squeezed and shaped her. Absorbed the hitch in her breath when he slid his palms down to her satiny thighs and pushed them apart.

"Colt—"

"Shh." Pressing a kiss to the small of her back, he slid his fingers underneath the sides of her flimsy panties and stripped them off.

Her breath grew shallower, her muscles tensing. "Relax," he whispered, stroking the inside of her thighs with a feather light touch. When she softened beneath his hands, he slid a pillow underneath her hips to raise her up. Spreading her thighs wider, he ran his knuckles along the soft, silky hair that covered her most intimate flesh. She shuddered, fingers grasping hold of the comforter.

He parted her with gentle fingers. Stroked her hot flesh from bottom to top.

She jerked beneath his hand. *"Colt."*

"Easy," he whispered in her ear, ghosting his thumb

over her. Again and again until she sighed, sank into it and pressed into his touch.

She grew softer, moister beneath his hand. Coating his fingers with her slick arousal, he eased two inside her. Her mewl of pleasure pushed him close to the edge.

He set his mouth to the hollow between her shoulder blades and pressed kisses to her skin while he worked his fingers in and out of her, keeping up a smooth, deep rhythm that had her climbing the rungs of a ladder he knew would lead to her release.

"God, Colt, please—"

Her body clamped tight around his fingers. Shifting lower, he spread her wide and put his mouth to her. Licked her with provocative, leisurely strokes while he worked her with his fingers.

"More," she begged.

He closed his mouth over the swollen nub at the center of her and sucked. *Devoured* her.

"You're so sweet," he rasped, drunk on the taste of her. "Come for me, angel."

She whimpered and lifted her hips. He drove his fingers hard inside her tight, hot warmth, his tongue nudging her core. She screamed, burying her face in the bedding, her earthy sounds of pleasure as her climax rode her the most arousing thing he'd ever heard.

He didn't stop until he'd made her come twice.

Her body racked with a series of aftershocks, Cecily stared up into Colt's beautiful dark eyes as he flipped her over.

Bracing a corded, insanely strong arm on the mattress beside her, he ran a finger down her cheek. "Live up to your expectations?"

Words stuck in her throat. She couldn't be droll in that moment. It had just been too…*earthshattering.*

His thumb slid to her mouth. He exerted a sensual pressure on her bottom lip until she opened to his caress. "Want to know what my fantasy is?"

Unsure she could take anymore, she forced herself to nod.

"You riding me," he murmured. "With all of that superior control and concentration of yours."

Her heart thudded in her chest. Dropping his hand from her mouth, he slid off the bed, stripped off his boxers and threw them on the floor. Her chest went tight. Full, heavy, so insanely masculine, just looking at him made her throb deep inside her core.

"I might like to redirect this fantasy," she murmured, eyes hot on him.

He pulled his wallet out of his jeans and extracted a foil package. "No," he said, coming back to her and tossing the condom on the bed. "You get yours," he murmured, sinking his fingers into her hips and lifting her on top of him, "and I get mine."

Twining a thick, golden curl around his finger, he brought her mouth down to his for a hot, devastating kiss that wiped any alternate plans from her head.

"You can put this on," he murmured when they came up for air. Curling his fingers around the foil package, he handed it to her.

"Oh." She gave him an uncertain look. "I'm not so good at that. My ex-fiancé and I—we—I was on the pill."

He didn't make fun of her. Didn't look down on her as Davis had for being so inexperienced. "Let me show you then."

He ripped the package open and took the condom out. Rolling it part way up his heartstoppingly virile length, he paused, capturing her fingers in his. "Now you."

Carrying her fingers to his shaft, he closed his hand over hers. Eased the condom up his pulsing flesh. Her breath hitched as he jerked beneath her touch. It was the most erotic thing she'd ever experienced.

"You're beautiful," she murmured, heart in her throat.

"Not like you," he said, shaking his head. A sensual promise lit his gaze. "Now get on me."

The stark, sexual command, the promise of oh, so much more pleasure, sent her pulse skyrocketing.

Lifting up on her knees, she curled her fingers around his shaft and brought the lush wide crest to her center. Empty, aching, the desire he inspired in her almost frightening in its intensity, she lowered herself onto the thick column of flesh, a moan tearing itself from her throat as she absorbed the power of him.

"Slowly," he murmured, eyes hot on hers. "You were made to take a man, angel."

Her stomach fell apart. Lost, immersed in a storm of her own making, sure nothing would ever compare to this moment, she had no choice but to surrender to it.

Slowly, gradually, her body gave around his, making way for his possession. When he was finally buried to the hilt, when she'd taken all of him, he uttered a curse, the hard lines of his face a study in concentration.

"Cecily," he murmured, his voice a rough caress, "*querida*. I need you to move, before I lose my mind."

He was holding back. On the edge. She dug her teeth into her lip, a flash of heat careening through her. That she could turn him on this much, that he desired her this greatly, healed a part of her she hadn't been sure would ever mend. It was a soul shaking moment she had to pause and fully absorb, bracing her palms on his rock-hard abs. For in that moment, they belonged to each other.

"Cecily…" Hoarse. Desperate.

She started to move, watching the pleasure explode in his eyes. The intimacy seemed too much, clawed at her to look away, but she couldn't, wouldn't, because if this was going to be her one night with Colt—she was going to remember every last second of it.

Her body fully aroused, drowning in the pleasure he was giving her, she took him easily now, sliding up and down his staff. He impaled her, touched her deeper every time she came down on him. Another orgasm built, this one slow moving and slumberous, radiating out from her core.

Colt tugged on her hand and pulled her forward. A palm at the small of her back, he arched her toward him and closed his mouth over a lace-covered nipple. She gasped, pushed herself deeper into his mouth. His cheeks hollowed out as he sucked her deep, sending more pleasure coiling in her abdomen.

"That feels so good," she moaned, moving faster on him now.

He switched his attention to her other nipple, teeth rasping across the tip as he drove up inside her, pushing so deep he set off a soul-shaking burst of pleasure that tore her apart.

Oh, dear God.

He cleaved his fingers through her hair and brought her mouth down to his. "I want your beautiful lips on mine when I come, angel. Your body is so sweet, you blow my damn mind."

Holding her bottom in his hands, he took her with sensual, mind blowing thrusts that sent more aftershocks of pleasure spiraling through her. Capturing her bottom lip between his teeth, he came with a throaty growl that reverberated right to her toes.

Seduced by his guttural sounds of pleasure, the hard stroke of his body, another wave of white-hot pleasure pulsed through her, rending her boneless and brainless, sprawled across his chest.

And then there was nothing but a dark, delicious abyss.

* * *

He woke her before dawn. Cupping her breast in his palm, he nudged her thigh forward and slid into her from behind.

"You wanted one night," he intoned huskily in her ear, "you get more."

His finger caressed the hard nub at the centre of her with smooth, delicious circles that soothed her sore skin. Rousing her desire all over again, he stroked her flesh until it was wet and pliant beneath his fingertips…until a low moan left her throat and she arched back against him, demanding his deeper possession.

He was in total control in this position. Exquisite and leisurely, as unhurried as the night before had been urgent, he made it last forever. A deep, delicious orgasm sliding over her, she curled back into his arms and slept.

When she woke again, her arms and legs tangled with Colt's, dawn had arrived. Hating to leave, but knowing she should before her absence was noticed and rumors spread like wildfire, she untangled herself and slipped from the bed.

Dressing in the pink-lit room, feeling like a very different woman than the one who had walked in here the night before, she let herself silently out the door and closed it behind her.

Shoes in her hand, feet soaked by the early morning dew, she ran up the path to the house.

All of a sudden, one night didn't seem like nearly enough.

Alejandro woke with a heavy head and a stinging jaw. Hitting the snooze button with the back of his hand, he pried his eyes open to find Cecily gone, the delicate floral scent that clung to the bedding the only evidence she'd even been there.

"Better like this," he muttered, dragging himself out

of bed and into a shower. He made it a practice never to let a woman sleep in his bed, which made awkward goodbyes a non-issue.

Returned to the land of the living with a hot shower, he found a text from Sebastien waiting for him when he got out.

Only a few hours left until you've successfully completed your challenge. The jet will be on the tarmac by eight o'clock this evening. You are leaving for personal reasons you must attend to immediately. Looking forward to hearing the debrief.

Santo Deus. He pocketed the phone and headed out the door. He needed out of here and *now*. Before he did something else he'd regret. Because surely what had happened between him and Cecily last night had been unwise. The problem was, he thought he might do it again if presented with the same situation, because watching that sexy confidence take up residence on her face as they'd blown each other's brains out in bed had been worth it.

He went about his daily chores, relieved to find Cecily and Dale had driven out of state to look at a horse after Knox Henderson's abrupt departure this morning. It was better he leave without goodbyes or explanations, because he had none to give.

No matter how real his feelings for Cecily—no matter how unfinished things between them seemed—*they* could never be. He had nothing to offer a vulnerable woman like her except what he'd just offered—a temporary boost to her ego.

The women in his life were well aware of who he was— knew they were temporary fixtures, to be pampered, enjoyed, then replaced as required. *Everybody won.* Cecily didn't fall into that category.

And then there was the fact that he was about to destroy her family's reputation. He was now convinced Cecily knew nothing of her horse's origins or the Hargroves' transgressions. But the crime still had to be punished. As soon as Stavros handed him the proof, he would secure justice for his grandmother just as he'd promised her he would.

Bacchus would be the only exception from the Salazar's revenge. Because on that point, he refused to break Cecily's heart.

CHAPTER FIVE

CECILY REACHED FOR the iron control she was famous for as she cantered into the ring in Geneva for her world championship qualifying event. She found herself deluged by nerves instead, her stomach churning like a rollercoaster ride.

Saluting the judges, she breathed in deep, gathered the electric charge of the crowd and used it to propel her around the course in a very fast, clean round—the final in the jump off.

She pulled Bacchus to a dancing halt, her horse sensing he'd been a star today. Staring up at the clock, heart in her mouth, the roar of the crowd echoed the numbers on the screen.

She had finished in third place.

It wasn't until Dale had pulled her off Bacchus in the collecting ring and engulfed her in a huge hug that it sunk in. *She'd done it*. Her world championship dream was still alive.

It wouldn't erase the lackluster year she and Bacchus had had, nothing could do that, but it would go a long way toward convincing the committee she should be in the running for a spot on the team. And right now, that was all she could do.

All due to Colt who'd found the key to her and Bacchus. A low throb pulsed through her as she pulled off her hat to greet the press. Colt who'd been gone when she'd returned from Maryland, a 'personal matter' drawing him home.

She'd been worried at first, asking Cliff for his phone number so she could make sure he was okay. But he hadn't left one. *As if what they'd shared had meant nothing to him.*

She kept the smile determinedly plastered across her face as she did half a dozen media interviews, wishing he were here. Which was ridiculous. She'd known he would leave. Had prepared herself for that. What had hurt the most was he hadn't even said goodbye.

Her stomach gave another ominous churn as she finished her last interview. Bile climbing the back of her throat, she barely made it to the washroom before she was violently ill.

It wasn't until she was on the jet flying home that pieces of the puzzle began sorting themselves into dizzying place. In the crush getting ready for Geneva, she hadn't had her period. She'd attributed it to stress, but *oh, my God.* Her heart seized as a sea of blue flew past outside the window. *It couldn't be.* Colt had worn a condom both times they'd made love.

A trip to her doctor, however, proved the impossible possible. She was pregnant with Colt's baby, a fact that threw her whole life—her career—into disarray once again.

Few top performing riders ever competed while pregnant. The risk wasn't worth it. Which meant there would be no world championships for her and Bacchus this year, the last thing she ever would have thought would derail her.

Shock and crushing disappointment consumed her as she fought her way through the next couple of days. What was she going to do? Her single, coherent thought was that Colt needed to know about his child. He might not want *her*, but it was his right to know they had conceived a baby together.

Finding him a preferable next step than telling her father she was pregnant with Colt's baby, she hired a private investigator who had tracked a fellow rider's birth mother down. Forty-eight hours later, Victoria Brown arrived at the coffee shop in town where Cecily had arranged to meet her, a manila folder in her hand.

Cecily lifted her gaze expectantly to the attractive brunette as she sat down, knots tangling her stomach.

"Did you find him?"

Victoria nodded. "There was a slight issue, however. Colt Banyon does not exist."

Cecily shook her head, confused. "But you just said you found him."

"I found the man who was posing as Colt Banyon." Victoria set her gray-blue gaze on Cecily. "There are no Banyons in New Mexico with any connection to the man who worked here. The man who worked for you fabricated his identity. A very sophisticated fabrication I might add."

Bemusement wrapped her brain in a gray haze. *Why would Colt do that? What had he needed to hide?* There had to be a logical explanation for it.

"I ran the photo you gave me from the party through my database," Victoria continued, "minus the facial hair. Colt's real name is Alejandro Salazar. He—"

The crash of china reverberated through the café, attracting stares from the clientele. Cecily looked down at the broken pieces of her cup littering the floor, then back up at Victoria, her brain frozen. *There must be some mistake.* It was not possible Colt could be Alejandro Salazar, the billionaire heir of her family's greatest rival. He could not have been working at Esmerelda.

There was no mistake, Victoria assured her as the girl from the shop came by with a broom to clean up her mess. She'd tracked Alejandro Salazar's movements during that time. He'd been in Kentucky. Colt *was* Alejandro.

She sat there in a daze after Victoria left, the world tilting on its axis. She was pregnant with *Alejandro Salazar's baby*. It was utterly, completely incomprehensible. She'd seen pictures of him of course, years ago, but he'd been clean shaven at a society event, nothing like the man who'd worked at Esmerelda.

Clasping her fingers around the new cup of tea the shop girl had insisted on bringing her, she fought to make sense of it all. What had Alejandro been doing here? Why had he been posing as a groom?

She'd never understood the ridiculous feud their two families were embroiled in. Had asked her parents about it multiple times only to be told the crazy rumors that Zeus's line had somehow been stolen from the Salazars were all in Adriana Salazar's delusional head.

Her heart dropped, fingers curling tight around the cup. Had Alejandro's presence here had something to do with that? Was he out to hurt her family?

Betrayal, hot and debilitating, slid through her. She'd thought she'd known him. That he'd cared about her. That he'd wanted her for who she was. When was she going to learn?

Davis had convinced her he'd wanted her too. She'd been so sure, so convinced he'd loved her she'd swanned all over town picking out china patterns, sending out rose-embossed wedding invitations, before she'd found out three weeks before the wedding from his drunken best man that her fiancé had a mistress he intended to keep. That instead of being the love of Davis's life, she had been a politically advantageous match chosen for her name and fortune.

Don't be so naïve, he'd raged at her when she'd broken things off. *Marriages have nothing to do with love.* Apparently she *had* been that naive, because it turned out she was the only one who hadn't seemed to know about her fiancé's dalliances.

Her teeth sank into her lip, the salt tang of blood staining her mouth. She'd promised herself she'd never let anyone hurt her that badly again. Use her that way. She'd let

Colt—*Alejandro*—in for the precise reason she'd believed he was different.

Once again, she'd been a *fool*.

She moved a numb gaze to the manila folder on the table. She should go home right now and tell her father. God knew what Alejandro Salazar's intentions were. But she couldn't do that—not with the explosive secret she carried. Not when her entire future depended on finding out what the truth was.

The only place she was going to find that was in New York.

CHAPTER SIX

"I HAVE YOUR PROOF."

Alejandro unfolded himself from his chair, stood, cell phone pressed to his ear and prowled to the floor-to-ceiling windows of his Manhattan office, a spectacular view of the Hudson River spread out before him.

"How accurate are your results?" he asked Stavros.

"Indisputable."

Satisfaction warmed his veins. "Courier them to me?"

"Already on the way." His friend took a sip of what was undoubtedly a double espresso served extra hot by his ever efficient PA. "Does this mean you'll have more time to devote to your friends now? At this rate it'll be Sebastien's thing before I see you."

Alejandro scowled. "It's his fault I'm so snowed under. If this damn party was anything but his anniversary celebration, I'd be saying thanks but no thanks."

"Aren't you even the least bit curious to meet my wife?"

Immeasurably. Meeting the woman who had somehow maneuvered Stavros into marriage was at the top of his personal priority list. Unfortunately, his hellish work schedule was derailing that plan.

"My curiosity will have to wait a couple of weeks."

"Kala." His friend took another sip of java. "I have a name to run by you. Guy by the name of Brandon Underwood—an old acquaintance of my wife's. He's in the race horse business."

Alejandro's lip curled. "Old money. Brandon's a spoiled rich boy with aspirations to follow in his senator daddy's footsteps. The Underwoods keep the rug swept so clean, you know there's dirt underneath."

"Good to know."

"You jealous of boy Underwood?"

"Hardly." Stavros shrugged the inquiry off as he always did anything that went more than surface deep. "You planning on bringing a plus-one to Sebastien's thing?"

He hadn't decided that yet. Given he was the only one flying solo, it had been tempting to pick up the phone and call the lawyer he'd met at the gym a few weeks ago, a beautiful brunette who'd made it patently clear she was waiting for his phone call. But he couldn't seem to do it.

Not even a vision of Brigitte's chic, chin-length bob, svelte figure and endless legs could strip his head of a certain voluptuous blonde who'd ridden him to within an inch of his life and left him wanting more. His body still seemed programmed for tiny, stacked females with an attitude.

"Might fly solo," he murmured absentmindedly, as his PA, Deseree, stuck her head in his office and gave him a five-minute signal. "I have a board meeting, I have to go. See you next week."

Stavros signed off. Pocketing the phone, Alejandro rifled through the papers on his desk. A frown creased his brow. "Des—" he called, walking to the door, "I can't seem to find that European market report. Can you scare up a—" the words froze in his mouth as he recognized the woman standing in front of his PA's desk.

Clad in a cream dress made of some soft material that hugged every memorable curve, a sky high pair of stilettos, her honey blonde hair a smooth silk curtain that fell over her shoulders, Cecily looked every bit New York chic. *Gorgeous.* But it was the icy glitter in her beautiful blue eyes that commanded his attention.

Por amor a Deus. She knew.

Dust in his throat, gravel in his mouth. *What the hell was she doing here?*

Deseree stared at them with unabashed fascination. He

snapped his stunned brain back into working order. He needed to defuse this…fast.

"Tell my father to start the meeting without me."

Deseree's jaw dropped. Salazar board meetings were a sacred thing. His father, Estevao Salazar, the Chairman of the Board, was known for his legendary temper tantrums over the tardiness of its members to his strictly laid out quarterly meetings. A true professional, however, Deseree didn't miss a beat, simply picked up the phone and started dialing.

Alejandro gestured toward his office. "After you."

Cecily turned on her heel and stalked inside. Her back a band of pure iron, fire sparking from every inch of her tiny frame, her amazing backside set off to perfection in the form fitting dress, she sent a wave of lust coursing through him that defied rationality. Now was *not* the time.

He closed the door with a soft click. Faced the firebrand in front of him. Hands clenched by her sides, a flush staining her cheeks, she was clearly furious. He thought he might start with an apology.

"*Eu sinto muito,* Cecily," he murmured, holding her gaze. *I'm sorry.* "I never intended to hurt you. I tried to take a step back, you know I did."

Eyes darkening, she lifted her hand and slapped him across the face. *Hard.*

"I deserved that," he said evenly, jaw reverberating with the force of it. "I deserve your anger. Now let's sit down and be rational about this. Let me explain."

"*Rational?*" She planted her hands on her hips. "You would like me to be *rational?* You came to work for my family under false pretenses. You lied to me and everyone else who trusted you, *cared* about you. You're lucky I haven't gone to the police."

He forced himself not to smile at how cute *police* came out in her feminine southern drawl. That would not help matters. "I haven't broken any laws," he returned smoothly. *Well, maybe one or two small ones.* "I applied for a job, was accepted and carried out my responsibilities."

"*Why?* What were you doing there?"

He leaned a hip against his desk. "Your family stole something from mine. I came to get proof."

She frowned. "Are you talking about *Zeus?* Does this have something to do with that crazy rumor you mentioned on our picnic?"

"It's not a rumor. Your grandfather illegally bred his mare Demeter to Diablo when Diablo was on loan to an American breeder, which means the whole backbone of your showjumping line is based on a lie. I have proof."

The color drained from her face. "What kind of *proof*?"

"I had Bacchus's DNA tested. He is irrefutably of Diablo's blood, not Nightshade's."

"I don't believe it," she whispered, skin a chalky white. "My parents told me it wasn't true."

"The testing was done in an internationally respected lab. There is no doubt as to its veracity."

She turned and walked to the window. Palm pressed to the glass, her slight shoulders stooped, body vibrating with emotion, he had to bite back the urge to touch her, to comfort her, because he couldn't do that anymore. He was the *enemy*.

She turned and leaned against the sill, those dark bruises in her eyes he hated. "Even if this is true, it happened *decades* ago. It's ancient history. Why can't you let it go?"

"Because your family stole something from mine and built a legacy around it. You profited immeasurably from it not only financially but in reputation, while I might add, throwing it in my family's face. It was a crime. It needs to be paid for."

Her mouth twisted. "Adriana is operating on bitterness. She and my grandmother had the biggest rivalry in the business. Adriana could never accept that my grandmother ended up on top. But she is *dead* now, Alejandro. There is no more skin to flay."

He lifted a shoulder. "Your family is still profiting from what it stole. My grandmother should have owned that glory. She will never rest until history is corrected."

"Why didn't she just move on?" She shook her head. "She had as many opportunities to breed Diablo as we did. Maybe we just did it better."

He flinched at the typically superior Hargrove response. "Diablo fell ill when he returned to Belgium." The words left his mouth on a scalpel's edge. "He was never able to sire any more offspring. Zeus was his last."

The blue of her irises expanded. Clearly she hadn't been privy to all the history—the depth to which her family had so completely destroyed his grandmother's legacy.

"What do you intend to do?"

"Take it to court. Extract all the damages my grandmother is due. Make it known the Hargrove legacy is built on a lie."

Her eyes darkened. "My father will never allow it. All it's going to do is create a media furor and drag both our family's names through the mud, only to be left with a truth that no longer means anything."

His blood heated. "It's a question of *honor*, something your family would have little idea of."

"Honor at what price?"

She looked so small, shaken, *vulnerable*, his heart contracted. "I've insisted Bacchus be left out of it. I will not see you two separated. That's the best I can do."

"How big of you." Her mouth curled. "You will save Bacchus while you destroy my family."

He studied her. Noted the dark shadows underneath her eyes. They were new—making her look even more bruised. Since he knew she'd finished in third place in Geneva, had checked the standings, he wondered why they were there. Why did she look as if a burst of air might blow her away?

"Why are you here?" he asked softly. "How did you know?"

"I hired a PI." She stared at him for a long moment, as if waging an internal battle, then losing the war as a breath escaped her. "Was any of it real? Who you are? The way we were together?"

It was his chance, he knew, to restore sanity to the situation. To cut this off now. To let her think it hadn't meant anything to him to make it easier for both of them in the long run. But he was as incapable of hurting her now as he had been from the beginning.

"Yes," he said matter-of-factly. "What we had was real, Cecily. But it was a mistake on my part. It never should have happened."

"That's right," she countered, hurt radiating in those big eyes. "I *begged* you to take me to bed and you are such a *man,* you kindly obliged me."

He took a step toward her. "That's not how it was."

She held up a hand, stopping him in his tracks. "Just to set the record straight—in case you think I was pining away for you, so *love struck* after that memorable night you gave me, I couldn't stay away—perhaps I should tell you the reason I hired a PI to find you. I am *pregnant*, Alejandro. How would you like to deal with that? How does that fit into this revenge plan of yours?"

His stomach dropped. "That's not possible. We used condoms."

"Condoms *fail*." Her expression was utterly flat. "Clearly they do because two pregnancy tests and a doctor have now confirmed it *is* possible."

His knees went weak. He wasn't about to question if it was his because he knew it was. Knew *her*.

The room swayed around him in a dizzying array of colors, his life as he knew it unraveling so fast it was like he'd lost control of the delicate rigging on his boat and was plunging fast toward a murky bottom.

"This is clearly a development we need to discuss."

Her eyes morphed to a deep, dark blue. "You think so? You intend on destroying my family, Alejandro. You lied to me from the first moment I met you. Why in the world would I have a civilized discussion with you about our baby? Seems to me, this conversation is over."

"Cecily—"

She backed up, eyes on his. "I don't even know who you are. How can I trust you with anything?"

Face shattering, she turned around, flung the door open and left.

Feeling as if a stiff whiskey was in order, Alejandro took himself to the executive conference room down the hallway instead, where the board meeting was in progress. But not before he dialed his driver and told him to follow Cecily when she left the building. Letting the little spitfire loose in New York with her explosive news wasn't a risk he was willing to take with a potential scandal in the making.

His father held court delivering the opening remarks as he slipped silently into his seat. Estevao Salazar stopped talking as he did, his piercing dark stare directed at his son. Alejandro ignored it and motioned for him to continue, head spinning too much to contemplate delivering the agenda.

"Soliciting unnecessary grief?" Joaquim murmured from beside him.

He gave his brother a black look, the irony of the remark sinking deep. *How could he have been so stupid to have risked something like this with Cecily?* He had told himself it wasn't a good idea to get involved with her. Had known the thin line he was walking. And what had he done? Let his lust and weakness for a blonde with big blue eyes and a vulnerable streak a mile-wide override his better judgment.

Maldita sea. Damn it to hell.

His father moved on to the first agenda item. He sat back in his chair. *This was a disaster.* Not an exaggeration when his grandmother refused to step foot in a room with a Hargrove. When Stavros had just delivered him the proof he needed to bring Cecily's family to its knees.

What was his family going to say when he casually announced he'd fathered a child with a Hargrove? What was Clayton Hargrove going to say when his daughter revealed she was pregnant with his child?

If he was in a mess, Cecily was in a worse one. She couldn't ride in the world championships now—at least she wouldn't if she were wise. A massive blow when she'd finally made it back to where she needed to be.

He wondered how she was handling it. Not well, he ventured, recalling her pale face. Those dark shadows ringing her eyes… She'd been carrying this around with her, no doubt trying to figure out what to do, his deception compounding the problem.

He shifted in his chair, the room feeling excessively hot. Loosened his tie. They would have this baby, of course. He might be one of the most commitment phobic creatures ever to roam this earth, but this was his *flesh and blood.* His heir. Becoming a father was a responsibility he would never shirk, particularly given the poor example his own had been.

Estevao Salazar had only ever been interested in raising a successor, not a son. His insatiable lust for power and the adulation that came with it had torn his family apart, his father's affairs driving Alejandro's mother across the ocean to pursue her riding career when their marriage disintegrated, leaving he and Joaquim to fend for themselves in their American boarding school.

His child, he knew with a bone-deep certainty, would have the love and stability he and Joaquim had never had in those early years before his grandmother had taken them in. They would never know a moment of the alienation and fear he had. Never doubt how much they were *valued*.

Which, he acknowledged, meant the right thing to do would be to marry Cecily. To provide his child with that stable environment he'd never had. It would cause waves, no doubt. His grandmother would lose her mind. But what else could he do?

He *liked* Cecily—admired her courage and strength. Their chemistry was undeniable. And since he'd never intended on marrying for love, since his vision had always been about practicality, about making that leap when the time came—well that time had clearly come.

Which didn't necessarily ease the haze enveloping his brain…the apprehension gripping his insides at having his life plan sped up by about five years.

His father pulled him aside on the break. Tall, still handsome at sixty with the smooth good looks he'd parlayed into a career of mistresses, Estevao Salazar's dark eyes snapped with irritation as he regarded his son.

"Nice of you to join us."

"My apologies. I had something urgent to take care of."

"Well see that it's taken care of before tonight. We have dinner with the Scandinavians. I want this deal done."

"I can't make it."

His father's gaze narrowed. *"Com licença?"* Excuse me?

Alejandro lifted a shoulder. "Take Joaquim. It's his deal. He can handle it."

A ruddy flush lit his father's cheeks. "What the hell is wrong with you, Alejandro? Where are your priorities? First your impromptu two-week vacation during our busy time, then *this*? What could be more important than this meeting?"

Avoiding a family scandal. Finding Cecily before she got on a plane.

"A personal matter." He met his father's fury with an even look. "Since you've had more than your fair share of those, I'm sure you'll understand."

Cecily paced her hotel suite, wondering what to do.

Perched high atop Madison Avenue, the luxury boutique hotel's Champagne Suite gave its occupant the impression of utter invincibility. But invincible was the last thing she felt at the moment. In fact, she was highly unbalanced from her showdown with Alejandro.

She should have come here with a plan. She needed a plan. But the fact was she had *no* plan, a problem when she was dealing with Alejandro Salazar, one of the world's most powerful men. Utterly in command of his domain today in his sky-high office, inherently sure of the power he wielded, he was clearly a lethally purposeful creature capable of doing whatever he needed to do to achieve his goal. *Which was to destroy her family.*

Not in the least bit hungry for the dinner she'd ordered, she crossed to the slate of windows that made up the entire front wall of the suite. Manhattan in all its glory sparkled back at her—a glittering spectacle so different from her beloved blue grass, she was usually entranced by it. But not tonight. Tonight nothing seemed to penetrate the numbness encasing her.

Her entire legacy had been built on a fabrication. Her parents had been lying to her this entire time. What it could mean for her family, her career, scared the hell out of her. To lose all her horses but Bacchus, to have the Hargrove name left in ruin. But there was another emotion present too…an insidious one that lingered at the edges. *Disappointment.*

She crossed her arms over the hollow feeling in her stomach. *What had she expected?* She'd known Alejandro wasn't *Colt*—the man she'd fallen for. Had known he was going to tell her something she didn't want to hear. She'd been through this before—the crushing disillusionment of finding out someone wasn't who they'd pretended to be. So what was the problem?

She'd wanted him to be that man who'd held and comforted her? Who'd made love to her so passionately as if it *meant* something? She'd wanted to be *wrong* about him? *God she really was a fool.*

His words echoed against the walls of her mind. *I tried to take a step back, you know I did.*

He was right. He had made every attempt to stay away from her—to demonstrate this thing between them wasn't wise. Had tried to cut things off time and time again. It had been *her* that had pursued him—*her* that wouldn't leave it alone—*her* that had seduced him.

He might have deceived her, but she held responsibility for this mess too.

A plan would have been helpful.

The peal of the doorbell jolted her out of her reverie. *Her dinner.* Pushing away from the window, she crossed the cream colored carpet on soundless feet, unbolted the door and pulled it open.

Alejandro, his sophisticated three-piece suit replaced by a pair of dark designer jeans and a red polo shirt, stood leaning against the door frame. Her heart hammered in her chest. His jaw smoothly shaven, sensual, forbidding mouth relaxed, dark eyes focused on her, he was no less intimidating than he'd been in the suit.

Pulse skittering, every cell affected by his blatant masculinity, she swallowed past the fist in her throat. "How did you find me?"

"I had my driver follow you."

Of course he had. She lifted her chin. "I told you, I'm done talking to you."

"If you were done talking you would have flown home this afternoon." His eyes glittered with a purposeful, black velvet cool. "We're having a child together, *querida*. We need to discuss what comes next. Or," he drawled, lifting a brow, "will you go home and casually mention to your father you're pregnant with my child with no game plan at all?"

"I hate you," she hissed. Particularly this new version of him.

"Go right ahead," he agreed in that smooth, reasonable tone. "But we still need to talk."

He was right. She stepped back, antagonism tightening every inch of her body. He strode past her into the suite, kicked off his custom-made Italian shoes and surveyed his surroundings.

"Nice suite."

"It was all they had to choose from." She watched as he walked to the bar and poured himself a whiskey. "Why don't you help yourself?"

"This is about six hours overdue," he murmured, picking up the glass, swirling its contents and taking a long gulp.

She wrapped her arms around herself as he lowered the glass and subjected her to one of those intense, utterly focused perusals of his. "Did you eat?"

"I have dinner on the way."

"Good. You look pale. You need to keep up your strength."

"Because I'm eating for two?" she scoffed. "You don't

have to pretend you care, Alejandro. My eyes are wide open now."

He cradled the glass in his palm, a ghost of a smile curving his lips. "I do care, Cecily. Thus the situation we find ourselves in. I told you that before I knew about the pregnancy. In fact, everything I said to you in Kentucky was true, every emotion I expressed real. The only thing I lied about was my identity and that I had to do."

Her stomach curled with the need to believe him. To believe *something* in all of this was real—that what they'd *shared* had been real. But she'd be a fool to take what he was saying at face value—even more of a fool than she'd already been.

He gestured toward the cream sofa that faced the spectacular view. "Why don't we sit down?"

"I'd prefer to stand."

"Fine." He lowered himself onto the chaise, splaying his long legs out in front of him. "We are keeping this baby, Cecily."

"Of course we are. *I* am," she corrected. "I would never do anything else."

"Good. And just to clarify," he drawled, eyes on hers, "when I said *we* are keeping this baby I meant *us*. We are both going to be parents to this child, which means we need to be *together* to do that."

She frowned. "What do you mean *together*?"

"I mean we will marry."

Her knees went weak. She slid down onto the sofa, a buzzing sound filling her ears. "You can't be serious."

"Oh, but I am." An amused smile twisted his mouth. "That's why I suggested you sit down."

Her heart beat a jagged rhythm. "You think we can base a marriage on a *lie*?"

"What we had wasn't a lie. We had something good—

you said so yourself…an organic connection it's impossible to manufacture."

"A connection you destroyed with your lies."

"A connection I *damaged* with my lies. I think we can repair it."

"How?" She lifted her chin. "I gave *Colt*—the man I thought I knew, my trust and *he* threw it away."

"I will earn it back," he countered. "The fact that you are carrying my baby changes everything, Cecily. I don't intend to give up my rights to this child and neither do you, which means we need to make this work. And since making this work means we need to smooth the way with our families, find a way to defuse this feud, *I* will begin the process."

"You said earlier your grandmother will never rest until she has her pound of flesh."

"If we present our relationship as a *fait accompli,* she will have no choice but to give." He frowned. "Perhaps she will be happy with an apology on the part of your family—some kind of public nod to the crime committed."

She shook her head. "My father will never agree to that. He would rather drag it through the courts for all eternity than tarnish the Hargrove name."

"Then he's a fool," he said harshly. "The Salazars could buy and sell your family ten times over. He would fight himself into the ground, only to lose."

She pressed her lips together. "You could make this concession regardless of whether we marry. We could find some peace between the two families and co-parent this child together."

His jaw hardened. "This child is a Salazar, Cecily. My heir. He or she will not be illegitimate."

The utter implacability behind that statement made her shoulders sag. "Even if we can negotiate our way through this family feud," she offered, "we hardly know one other. What's to say we can even make this work?"

"Chemistry is ingredient number one for a good relationship." His gaze speared hers, so familiar and yet so foreign. "We have proven we have that, both in bed and out of it. We have also proven we can be a great team. What more could you ask for?"

Love? That elusive thing she craved but wasn't sure actually existed. For her at least.

"Practicality," Alejandro murmured, sensing her hesitation, "is the thing to base a marriage on. Not this creative storytelling everyone is trying to sell these days of happily-ever-afters that don't exist."

"My parents were in love," she said quietly. "That's why he is the way he is, my father. Because he's never gotten over her."

"Isn't it better to avoid that completely? To base a relationship on pragmatism and affection instead?" He shook his head. "I won't lie and promise you things I don't believe in, Cecily. But I do believe we can make this work. Think about how good we were in Kentucky."

She didn't want to think about that because she wasn't sure if any of it had been real. That he wasn't playing her right now to get what he wanted in his child. Except, she acknowledged, swallowing past the tightness in her throat, it was impossible to forget how patiently he had helped her and Bacchus reconstruct their relationship. How he had helped her reconstruct *herself* in those difficult weeks they'd spent together.

She studied the hard, uncompromising lines of his face. Could he really have manufactured the depth of caring he'd displayed? Why would he have when really, there'd been no reason for him to do it—every reason to do the opposite in fact?

"Why did you help me with Bacchus?" she asked.

JENNIFER HAYWARD   91

"I couldn't stand to watch you hurt," he said quietly. "Even though I told myself it was a bad idea, even though I tried to make myself immune to you, you got under my skin."

Her heart contracted. Emotions, feelings, she'd convinced herself had been a figment of her imagination, a product of her naiveté, flooded back in a storm of confusion. She would have preferred the cold, hard truth to this gray area she couldn't process.

She pushed to her feet and walked to the windows, staring out at the lights dripping from the skyscrapers like tear drops hanging from their tall, imposing perches.

"This is insanity."

"You aren't in this alone, Cecily. I'm here."

He who had never intended on saddling himself with a wife in this revenge plan of his...a notorious bachelor by anyone's standards.

She turned around and rested her palms on the sill. "What about all the women you seem to possess for every different social occasion? I'm supposed to believe you will simply give up your bachelorhood to marry me because of our baby?"

He smiled, that whiskey-colored glimmer that did funny things to her insides lighting his eyes. "I find I like the idea of you as a wife. We would never be short of fireworks. I'm sure it would be more than enough to prevent me from straying."

His arrogance hit her right in the solar plexus, right where Davis had torn her heart out. "*If* I am crazy enough to agree to marry you," she stated icily, "which is doubtful at this point, I will not tolerate infidelity. Any hint of it and I walk."

His gaze narrowed. Rolling to his feet, he covered the distance between them. "It was a joke," he murmured. "My father is a serial affair artist. I would never do that to my own relationship."

"That was the truth then, what you said that night about your parents' dysfunctional relationship?"

"All of it was the truth." His gaze held hers. "Now do you want to tell me why you have that look on your face?"

She shook her head. No way was she offering him her truths when he had withheld his.

"Fine. But you *will* tell me, Cecily, because we are going to repair these trust issues of ours."

She sank her teeth into her lip, feeling far too vulnerable, fragile like glass. "If I were smart," she breathed, "I would be getting on a plane right now and flying home, because *this* is not rational. I should not trust you."

"But you do," he countered softly. "You have from the beginning. You know *me*, Cecily. Trust me now. Do this with me."

A haze of indecision clouded her brain. "I need time," she rasped. "To process this. To figure out what to do."

"Fine. You have a week."

"*A week?*"

"It's too explosive a situation to prolong. My grandmother wants action taken. Plus," he added, "I am due to attend an anniversary party in England at the end of the month. If we are to be married, you should be the woman on my arm."

"You mean you don't already have one lined up?" She hated the sharp claws of jealousy that scored her insides. "I would have thought they'd be chomping at the bit to be at your side."

"Funny that," he murmured, eyes on hers. "I was having trouble getting a certain blonde out of my head. I kept remembering how she wrapped herself around me and took me for the ride of my life...those sexy moans she made when I took her apart...how *sweet* she tasted when I did." His eyes were hot, black velvet now. "I find I want *more*."

Her insides fell apart, a wild heat invading her cheeks. A satisfied smile curved his mouth. "We are good together, *querida,* you know we are. Now you just need to admit it."

She lifted her hands to her burning cheeks. "I am not going to make a decision based on our…*sexual compatibility.* That would be foolish."

"Then make it based on rationality. Your life has imploded around you, Cecily. You need me to take control and fix this. *We* need to make a home for this child. It is the only solution."

A flustered denial bubbled to her lips. It died in her throat when he picked up his glass, drained its contents and walked to the door.

"Make a decision," he said, swinging around to face her, "and let me know."

And then he was gone.

CHAPTER SEVEN

CECILY FED A chilled-out Bacchus the last handful of his favorite breakfast treat as she stood perched on the bottom rung of the pasture fence on a gorgeous, sun-soaked day at Esmerelda.

Clearly enjoying his sojourn from his intensive training schedule, her horse was utterly content grazing with his pasture mates. His mistress, however, was still fighting the crushing disappointment of watching her dream go up in smoke.

This morning, she'd called the head of the decision making committee to let him know about her pregnancy—that she wouldn't be competing for a world championship team spot. It had killed her to do it—worse when he'd given her no idea if she'd have been chosen or not, a nudge of confidence she'd sorely needed in that moment.

And still she hadn't told her father.

A whisper of apprehension fluttered in her belly. She needed to do that today, because today was the deadline Alejandro had given her to make up her mind on whether she would become his wife. A *Salazar*.

She knew what her decision had to be—she'd just been too afraid to voice it.

She couldn't bring up this baby alone, not after she'd lost her own mother so young. Not when that void would always be with her and she wouldn't do that to her child. Nor could she simply stand by and watch her legacy destroyed, her beloved horses taken away, everything her mother and grandmother had accomplished wiped away in a red stain of disrepute. Because Alejandro would win this battle—she knew he would.

Which left her with only one option: to marry him. He'd already been as good as his word, flying to Belgium this week to convince his grandmother to accept a public apology on the part of the Hargroves as compensation for her family's crime. Then he'd followed that up with a call to sweeten the pot. Marry him and he would buy them a property in upstate New York where she could build her dream stables away from the oppressive presence of her father.

A generous gesture of goodwill, a tempting one at that, but it couldn't buy her trust. That he would have to earn.

She bit her lip as she considered a brilliant, clear blue Kentucky sky. Her choice might be clear but none of it negated her fears of picking up her life and plunking it down in New York as Alejandro's society wife. The thought of leaving her home was unbearable. She simply didn't think she had any choice.

She gave Bacchus a final scratch behind the ears and headed for the house and the inevitability that lay ahead. The door to her father's study was closed. About to turn away, deep male voices raised in anger froze her feet in place.

Alejandro's voice.

He couldn't have. Wouldn't have.

Breaching the social etiquette that had been drilled into her since birth, she turned the handle on the door and let herself inside the leather and cigar-infused room. Her father, dressed in casual slacks and a shirt, stood toe-to-toe with Alejandro who looked gorgeous in a navy suit and ice-blue tie.

Her heart thumped wildly in her chest as her father turned a freezing gray gaze on her. "Tell me it isn't true," he rasped.

She swallowed hard, knees weak. "What isn't true?"

"That you are pregnant with his child."

She wrapped her arms around herself, throat tight.

"Yes," she said quietly, looking her father in the eye. "I am. I was going to tell you today. Alejandro clearly beat me to it."

"Today?" her father bellowed. "You knew he came here under false pretenses. Knew what he was planning and you didn't tell me? What were you—so caught up in him you were blind?"

Her anger caught fire. "*You* knew about Zeus. About Bacchus... You lied to me, Daddy."

"I was protecting you from *their* lies," he roared. "How could you be so stupid as to do this? I thought I raised you with some sense in your head."

Alejandro stepped to her side and slid an arm around her waist. "I think you should watch how you're talking to your daughter," he said evenly.

"Stay out of this." Her father kept his gaze trained on her. "The Salazars are out to ruin our name and you are playing right into their game."

"Granddaddy already did that. He broke laws doing what he did. He *stole* from them."

"It never happened. Adriana has never been able to get past her jealousy at Harper's success, at *our* success, so she chooses to try and tarnish our name with her crazed ramblings."

"Alejandro has proof. The truth needs to come out, Daddy. No more lies."

Her father turned to Alejandro. "I want you off my property. *Now*. We will settle this in court."

"You are being shortsighted," Alejandro drawled. "Take what my grandmother is offering... It's the best you're going to get. Make a public apology and put this all behind us."

Her father scowled. "You think I would risk a century-old dynasty offering the Salazars an apology for something that never happened?" He shook his head. "I will tie this up in legalities forever. It will never see the face of a courtroom."

Cecily's heart sank. If it wasn't true what her grandfather had done, there would be no need to stall a court case because the truth would come out.

What else had her father been lying to her about?

Alejandro's fingers tightened against her back. "You are willing to trade your daughter's happiness to perpetuate a lie? If you keep this up, Clayton, there will never be peace between our two families and your grandchild will be stuck in the middle."

"No it won't," her father disagreed. "The courts will give Cecily custody. They always rule in favor of the mother."

"That may be the case," Alejandro rebutted coolly, "but it's inconsequential because Cecily is going to marry me."

Her father's face went a deep shade of gray. "That can't possibly be true."

Furious at both men, Cecily would have loved to have told both of them to go to hell. But she'd made her decision. This baby was going to grow up with both its parents.

"It's true," she confirmed. "I am going to marry Alejandro. So you, Daddy, need to wrap your head around ending this feud."

Clayton Hargrove's jaw hardened. "No daughter of mine is marrying a Salazar. You walk out that door with him and you cut your ties with this family."

Her stomach lurched. "You don't mean that."

Her father crossed his arms over his chest. "Stay and we'll work through this. Leave and you are on your own."

Alejandro lowered his head to hers. "Go pack a bag. You can send for the rest of your things later."

She blinked. "You want me to leave with you *now?*"

"Do you want to stay?"

One look at her daddy's face convinced her that no, she did not. She'd made her decision. She needed to go.

* * *

Alejandro spent the flight back to New York stickhandling the two deals he had up in the air after his whirlwind trip to Belgium and Stockholm—the Scandinavian tie-up he'd been negotiating with Joaquim and the acquisition of a twenty-five billion dollar Columbian coffee company Salazar had been lusting after for decades.

He thought it a good thing Cecily had some time to cool down with a parade of drivers, passport officials and flight attendants providing a buffer between them. She was clearly furious with him, in one of her patented snits, when all he'd been trying to do was help given how wary she'd sounded about approaching her father.

Having scaled three countries in forty-eight hours cleaning up the mess *she* had had an equal hand in creating, he was not in the mood. Not after his confrontation with his grandmother in which she had accused him of a lack of judgment, of *loyalty,* when he'd told her about his relationship with Cecily.

His knuckles gleamed white as he snapped his laptop shut with more force than necessary. They had cut right through him those words, coming from the woman who had taught him the meaning of honor—who'd been the guiding force in his life. For her to question his loyalty had both gutted and infuriated him, made worse by the fact that he'd been forced to lie to her about being in love with Cecily in order to bring some sanity to the situation.

His grandmother had, nonetheless, grudgingly agreed to make the compromise he'd asked of her—the offer Clayton Hargrove had so foolishly rejected. He could only hope Cecily's father had the sense to come around.

His fiancée, unfortunately, was no calmer by the time they got home. She turned on him the minute they'd walked through the door of his architecturally striking, five-story Upper East Side townhouse, blue eyes blazing.

"Why did you do that?" she erupted. "You just made everything worse."

"It's going to be fine," he murmured soothingly, shutting the door. "I promise you. Your father will cool down, I will bring your horses to New York, we will find a place to keep them and we will have a good life together."

"I just don't understand," she raged, as if she hadn't heard him. "Is your head so thick you didn't think I'd know the right way to handle this?"

His jaw clenched. "Then why haven't you? What were you doing, waiting for divine inspiration…for the muses to give you the green light? Perhaps if your father had already absorbed the shock of your pregnancy, he would have been better able to consider my offer."

"I was going to tell him after I talked to you. I would have *eased* him into it. But no, you had to fly in like a big hotshot and call all the plays."

"That's not what I was doing," he said silkily, temper beginning to fail. "I'm stretched to the limit as I seek to solve our dilemma, *querida*. I was trying to help. Forgive me if I neglected to use the finesse you so clearly desired."

She blinked. "How could you possibly be *helping*?"

"You sounded unsure about telling your father. I thought if we handled it together it would be better."

"You handled it by *yourself*," she growled. "You have no sensitivity. A typical male."

Por amor a Deus. He ran a hand through his hair. Was this what his marriage was going to be? One argument after another? The very thing he'd promised himself it would never be.

He understood she was upset, that her life had been blown apart, but so had his. *He was marrying her, for God's sake.* He was going to be a *father*. If he wasn't so busy he might be experiencing a severe case of "free market pre-withdrawal" withdrawal.

"And then," she bit out, on a roll now, "you had the audacity to assume I was going to accept your marriage proposal before I even gave you my answer."

"But you *were*," he came back evenly. "Just out of curiosity, why did you?"

She crossed her arms over her chest. "My mother died when I was fourteen. I spent my most formative years without a female influence. I will never deprive my child of its father."

"Then we both agree that putting our child first is what this is all about."

She gave a reluctant nod.

"Along that vein," he suggested pleasantly, "let me give you a tour of your new home. I think you're going to love it here."

"I will never love New York," she said flatly. "Not like I love Kentucky. I mean it's exciting and all, but I feel like I can't *breathe* here."

"You can, I assure you. I do it every day." He flicked a wrist toward the living room. "After you..."

He gave her a tour of the luxury residence he'd paid twenty-three million for—through the dramatic, double-height living room with its twenty-foot ceilings, exposed brick walls and fireplace, to the magnificent dining room built to entertain.

He thought perhaps the private nanny quarters, the yoga studio or the multi-level roof garden might win her over, but Cecily remained stone-faced throughout the tour. He abandoned his enthusiasm when they reached the top floor master bedroom suite with its massive arched windows and wood burning fireplace, leaving her to freshen up before dinner.

He must've been insane to ever contemplate this marriage. Not only was his soon-to-be wife *persona non grata* with his family, she was so far from the practical solution he'd envisioned, it was like ending up with a custom-made, extremely temperamental sports car when all you'd really wanted was a sleek-looking sedan.

Cecily knew she was being a shrew, but she was so angry at Alejandro for what he'd done, so sideswiped by the events of the day, she thought it better to say nothing at all than let loose with something she shouldn't.

By the time they sat down to dinner on the terrace, she thought she had gotten her emotions firmly under control. A serene, stunning oasis with its hidden nooks and vibrant landscaping, the outdoor space was a slice of heaven in the middle of New York City.

It went a long way toward soothing her raw edges, a good thing because sitting across from Alejandro dressed in jeans and an old Harvard T-shirt, his hair mussed, feet bare, didn't exactly put her in a relaxed frame of mind. He was just *that* gorgeous and looked far too much like the man she'd fallen for in Kentucky.

"Why this?" she asked, waving a hand around them as his housekeeper, Faith, removed their salad plates and brought them coffee and tea. "Why a home instead of some big shot bachelor penthouse from which you can rule the world?"

His ebony eyes sparked with warning. "I think that's enough with the big shot comments, *meu carinho*. You are twenty-five, not five, no?"

She sat back in her chair, cheeks hot. Maybe she hadn't quite reacquired her powers of control.

"The house," he elaborated, "was a surprise for me. I was planning on buying something easier to maintain, then my agent showed me this." He lifted a shoulder. "Maybe it was so many years spent in boarding schools, being shuffled between Brazil and Belgium with my parents living apart. I found I liked the idea of a home."

She absorbed the information about the man she really knew nothing about, which was disconcerting to say the least when he had been privy to her most intimate thoughts and feelings.

"Where did you go to school?" she asked, in an attempt to rectify that.

"New Hampshire." He sat back, coffee cup balanced on his thigh. "My parents sent me to an elite boarding school when I was six. The plan was always to build up Salazar's US operations, so having me and my brother in the States made sense. My father was always traveling and my mother spent most of her time on the road pursuing her equestrian career in Europe."

Six. Her heart contracted. She'd always thought the boarding school concept was inhumane, but that was *so* young.

"It must have been difficult to live so far away from your family."

"It was all Joaquim and I knew. Life at home was hellish—we preferred to be at school. We had each other. And in the summers and on school holidays, we'd be at the farm in Belgium with my grandmother."

She sank her teeth into her lip. Absorbed the hard, impenetrable lines of his face. She had the feeling the emotionally closed-off Colt she'd come to know in Kentucky was very much the man sitting across from her—one shaped by his earliest, most painful experiences.

She took a sip of her tea. Regarded him from over the rim of her cup. "What happened with your parents' marriage? Were they ever in love?"

"Madly so, according to my grandmother. It was a passionate, wild, emotional rollercoaster of a ride until my father's attention wandered a few years after Joaquim was born. Not an unusual occurrence in the society we lived in, but my mother, as you can imagine from her ambitious career, was not the type to turn a blind eye.

"She raged at him, threatened to divorce him and when neither worked, embarked on a series of affairs designed to win him back. But none ever did. Eventually she gave up and moved full-time to Belgium for her riding career, neither dissolving the marriage nor pursuing it because the arrangement worked."

Leaving her children behind in the process. "What's your relationship with your parents now?"

"My father and I have never been close. His focus has always been on the business to the exclusion of everything else. My mother—" his face assumed a neutral expression, "is…delicate. She withdrew into herself after the separation, focusing on her riding and her teaching. It would not be a stretch to say she knows some of her students better than she knows Joaquim and I."

Her chest tightened. She knew that sense of alienation—the pain that came with being distanced by someone you loved. Her father had withdrawn into himself after her mother's death with nothing, it seemed, to give to her.

"That couldn't have been easy," she said quietly, "having such a childhood."

"Thus my deep, dark, damaged views on love?" His mouth twisted. "It was actually a relief when my parents separated for good. My mother was happier that way. Things became civil. The tension was gone. It made me see how a practical marriage like the one you and I are about to embark on can work. Everyone's happy…no one gets hurt."

She wondered if that could be true. If the practical union she had agreed to with Alejandro was a better choice than her deeply held desire to be loved? After what she'd gone through with Davis, she couldn't be sure it wasn't.

"Practical, however," Alejandro continued, "will not do for my grandmother. The only way I could extract the concession I did from her was to make her believe we are madly in love—that *we* and this child are a foregone conclusion. She is anxious to meet you and hear about our wedding plans. I told her we'd stop in on the way home from England."

Wedding plans? Meeting Adriana? Her stomach folded in on itself. "I can't even think about a wedding until my father comes around. I always imagined it would be at Esmerelda."

"Then an early October date will give him incentive to see reason."

Her jaw dropped. His expression remained firm. "I'm not so concerned people will know our child has been conceived out of wedlock. I do, however, intend for us to be married when it happens."

A tumble of words rose to her lips. "But that's two months away," she finally managed. "We can't plan a wedding that quickly."

"You will have people to do it for you."

Dear God. She stared at him. "And how are we to handle the news of our baby in public? At this anniversary party, for instance. I think it's too soon to talk about it."

"Agreed. Removing it from the equation also increases the likelihood people will buy this is a love match. Which," he underscored, "is something we need to accomplish in England. It will be a very high profile party—anyone who's anyone will be there—lots of paparazzi. As our public debut together, it will be our chance to send a clear message to everyone, including your family and mine, that this union is real. That they have no choice but to accept it."

A knot formed in her chest, all of it much too much all of a sudden. Perhaps it was the whirlwind wedding he was demanding…the baby she wasn't ready for…the emotionally explosive day it had been. Or perhaps it was that only a few weeks ago she'd been head over heels for the man she'd thought he was. When acting as if she'd had feelings for him—carrying out this charade—wouldn't have been an issue—it would have been a reality.

"Speaking of babies," he said, pouring himself another cup of coffee from the carafe, "my PA has made you an appointment with the best OBGYN in Manhattan. Better you initiate that relationship now so you can build on it as you go."

So he could ensure the Salazar heir was healthy and well protected more likely. It was, after all, the reason she was here.

She fell quiet as a violet light descended over Manhattan, such a different canvas from the star-infused, inky-black sky she was used to, she was suddenly, achingly homesick.

Alejandro set his cup on the table. "It's late. You look exhausted. You should go to bed. I'll join you in a few minutes after I send a couple of emails."

Her shoulders stiffened at yet another order, but she *was* exhausted. She climbed the stairs to their bedroom, barely able to put one foot in front of the other.

Did he expect her to share his bed? She thought the answer might be yes as she arrived in the sumptuous master suite to find Faith had put her clothes away in the armoire while they had eaten, her toiletries laid out neatly in the opulent, marble and limestone en suite.

She stared at them, not sure she was ready for this. Sure, in fact, she wasn't.

Immersing herself in a cool shower, she attempted to regain her equilibrium. But her nerves grew with every moment that passed. Eventually she *would* have to share that bed with Alejandro—to get to know the complex, intimidating male she'd agreed to marry on every level. But she needed to trust him again first.

She understood from their conversations the deep sense of honor that drove him, *why* he'd done what he'd done, could even accept he'd tried not to hurt her, but he'd damaged them in the place she was the most vulnerable by deceiving her and that was not going to be easy to forgive.

Clad in her favorite pale pink nightie, she brushed her hair in the black stone mirror that lay as an accent piece against the wall in the bedroom, her pulse a staccato drumbeat in her throat.

Alejandro walked in moments later. Eyes wary, face lined with fatigue, the same dark stubble shadowing his jaw he'd worn at Esmerelda, he undid his sleek gold watch and set it on the dresser.

His visible exhaustion unearthed a twinge of guilt. "I'm sorry," she said quietly, "for my behavior today. I'm not myself. I'm overwhelmed, turned upside down. I don't know which way is up anymore."

His expression softened. Dropping his cufflinks on the dresser, he moved behind her, setting his hands on her hips. She jumped, the heat of his touch burning into her skin. He settled his hands more firmly around her. "Try and relax," he said softly. "I never renege on a promise, Cecily. I will make this right."

"What if he never calls—my father?" Her gaze met his in the mirror. "What if he doesn't come around? Things haven't always been good between us but he and my horses are all I have."

"He will. He loves you. And," he murmured, "you have me now—the life we will build together. Think of this as your chance to be something other than a Hargrove, to be what *you* want to be—everything we talked about in Kentucky. I said I would back you one hundred percent and I will."

Warmth surged through her. For the first time today, she almost believed it, that everything would be okay, because this man's will would accept nothing less.

This was the man she'd fallen for in Kentucky. Was *he* somewhere within this arrogant stranger she'd agreed to marry?

He took the brush from her hand and laid it on the dresser. "You were right," he said softly, "that I didn't wait for your answer—that I simply assumed you would become my wife. That said, I hope this will make up for the lack of a romantic proposal."

Her throat went dry as he captured her left hand and slid a ring on her finger. Perched on a delicate platinum band, the round, brilliant-cut diamond was cast in a halo setting, accented by hundreds of tiny diamonds that flashed in the light.

It was the most beautiful thing she'd ever seen.

"I thought it fit your vibrant personality," he murmured. "But if you don't like it, I can have Jovan make something else."

Didn't like it? He'd had it made for her? She melted.

"It's perfect," she said huskily. "Exactly what I would have chosen. Thank you."

He feathered a thumb across her palm, keeping her hand tucked in his. "You need to be wearing the appropriate rock when you walk into that party with me. I think this will do the trick."

She stiffened, the glow inside her evaporating. *For goodness sake, Cecily, get a grip. Remember what this is.*

"It's perfect." She pulled her hand free, channeling the ice princess persona she did so well. "I think you're right, actually. I need some sleep. I'm sure I'll feel better in the morning."

"Why not now?" His throaty rejoinder unraveled a curl of heat inside her as he bent to bring his mouth to her ear.

"We're engaged now, *querida*. There's no reason to hold back."

A flood of seductive, heady memories swamped her senses. She pushed them ruthlessly away. She was his *convenient* wife—the one bearing him his child—nothing more. Just like she'd been for Davis. Paramount to surviving this relationship was going to be keeping her head where he was concerned.

"Yes there is." She twisted out of his arms and turned to face him. "We need time to ease into this, Alejandro. For me to learn to trust you again. For me to get to know *who* you are."

He frowned. "You *know* who I am. We've talked about intimate things…deep things. That *is* who I am."

"I *thought* I knew you," she corrected. "Now I'm not sure what to believe."

He stared at her for a long moment, jaw tight. "Fine. Take all the time you need. But the image we present in public is non-negotiable. We *will* look madly in love at that party even if you have to channel your best acting job to do it. Are you clear on that?"

"Crystal," she murmured. "I'll start practicing right now."

CHAPTER EIGHT

ALEJANDRO SPENT THE next two weeks working day and night to free himself up for his trip to England, his multi-billion-dollar acquisition occupying the lion's share of his time. Aware that his fiancée was swimming in the deep end and doing her best to stay afloat, he brought work home with him and had dinner with her each night rather than cast her adrift in Manhattan.

Which also allowed him to work toward his other goal of proving to Cecily she could trust him. That he was that man she'd known in Kentucky. He found himself sharing pieces of himself he rarely did in an effort to have his fiancée do the same with him. It was going to take time, but slowly, ever so gradually, she was letting down her guard. He was beginning to see glimpses of the woman he'd first gotten to know—the open, vulnerable Cecily she was at the heart of her.

It infuriated him that her father hadn't called with an olive branch. As if he truly meant to take the Hargroves' crime to the grave with him rather than allow it to tarnish the family name. As if he cared more about his legacy than the daughter he'd disowned.

It was tearing Cecily apart—he could see it in her expressive blue eyes when her vulnerability shone through. Seeking to provide her with a distraction, he pushed ahead with his plans to buy them a place in upstate New York. While his real estate agent searched for the ideal property, he had Cecily work with an architect to envision what her dream stables would look like. Not only had it occupied his fiancée, it had put a sparkle back in her eyes and given them a project they could work on together.

By the time they boarded the Salazar jet for the anniversary party, they had developed a workable rapport between them. Her continuing to freeze him out was another matter. It wasn't going to work this weekend with the façade they had to perpetuate, nor was it going to close the gulf that had grown between them. And since eliminating that tension, putting his life back into its pre-Kentucky order, was his number one priority right now, he needed to solve *her*.

Watching her now, curled up in a chair beside him as the jet leveled out into a smooth sea of blue, he felt that familiar tug of desire. Dressed in leggings and a sweater that emphasized her soft curves, her legs curled beneath her as she reviewed the architect's revamped drawings, it was as if she flicked some internal switch inside of him just by being in the same room.

What would she look like when she started to show evidence of their child? He imagined those lush curves grown ripe with his son or daughter, a powerfully possessive feeling assailing him, one he couldn't even begin to articulate. She would be even more desirable, if that was possible.

He ran a palm over his jaw. Sexual frustration was not, he was discovering, a state of being he enjoyed.

"Happy with them?" he asked, nodding at the drawings.

She nodded. "They're getting there."

"Bring them over. Show them to me."

She uncurled herself from the chair and perched on the arm of his, walking him through the drawings. They were impressive. She'd thought of everything: roomy, loose boxes for every horse in the barn, extra wide aisles for grooming, a bathing area done in tile as well as multiple indoor and outdoor schooling rings that took into account the cold New York weather. Eventually, he knew, she wanted to be a coach, helping younger riders just as her mother had done.

He pointed to one of the outdoor rings. "You might want

to put that one next to the ring for the more mature horses. The novices tend to pick up their good habits."

She chewed on her lip. "That's a good idea." She made a note. Asked if he had any more thoughts. Because he loved the subject, he did, suggesting small refinements here and there. When they were done, she rolled up the drawing and stayed put.

"Tell me about your friends," she prompted quietly, "so I'm not walking into this cold."

Something he should have done already, but hadn't in his preoccupation with everything on his plate. He captured her hand in his, smoothing his thumb over her palm. "I have three close friends. Sebastien Atkinson founded the extreme sports club we all joined in college. It's he and his wife Monika's anniversary party we're attending.

"Stavros," he continued, "is in pharmaceuticals, based here in New York." His mouth curved. "He's a piece of work. You'll see what I mean when you meet him. He recently married a Greek woman named Calli I haven't met yet, so you won't be the only new face."

"Did they elope?"

"Something like that. Antonio," he concluded, "owns one of the world's largest construction companies. Italian, very charming, easy to like. He recently married the mother of his son. A child he didn't know about," he qualified, "until just a few weeks ago."

She frowned. "Why is that?"

"Leo is the product of an old affair between he and Sadie. Why she didn't tell him about his son, I don't know. I expect I'll find out more when I see him."

She nodded. Shifted her weight to stand up. He sank his thumb deeper into the flesh of her palm to keep her there. Heat darkened her eyes, that always on electricity pulsing between them, but there was a wariness there too, a seemingly permanent state of affairs he was beginning to hate, particularly when he'd been the one to put it there.

"I will clearly have to kiss you this weekend," he said huskily. "Perhaps we'd better get back into practice?"

She froze, the hesitancy written in every bone of her body making him curse beneath his breath. He was demonstrating she could trust him in every way he could. *What the hell more could he do?*

"Alejandro…"

"Forget it." He pushed the drawing back at her. "I've got work to do."

He was in a fairly antagonistic mood then as they arrived at Sebastien's glorious Waldenbrook estate in Oxfordshire, situated on two hundred acres of lush, green, forested land.

Perhaps Sebastien would offer up one of his sadistically cruel, military-inspired obstacle courses this weekend… some target practice with a powerful gun. *That* could burn off some frustration.

"Not this weekend." Sebastien dashed his hopes as he stood on the front steps of the impressive Georgian manor, his arm wrapped around his wife. "My niece, Natalia, is mad about show jumping. We're hosting the Oxfordshire County Show this weekend as a show of support."

Alejandro scowled. *A horse show?*

His disappointment evaporated when he saw Cecily's pale face. *Meu Deus. Of all the weekends.* Sebastien moved his gaze between the two of them. "Of course." He bumped his head with his hand. "How bloody stupid of me. Of course you should ride, Cecily. I should have let you know. Borrow one of Natalia's horses."

Cecily pushed a smile to her face. "I'm taking a break from riding. Just for a short while with the engagement and my move to New York."

"Well you must come out and cheer for Natalia. She'd be so thrilled."

His fiancée didn't flinch even though they'd announced the American world championship team today, the papers full of the news, rife with speculation as to why she hadn't made it. Instead of focusing on her brilliant comeback in Geneva, the press had noted Cecily's less than stellar year. He knew it was killing her but she didn't let it show.

"I would enjoy that," she murmured. "Of course."

Sebastien sent them off to get settled in their room before cocktails, a staff member carrying their luggage.

"I didn't know," Alejandro said in a low voice.

Cecily lifted a shoulder. "It's fine."

It wasn't fine. Cecily attempted to readjust her bearings as she and Alejandro were shown to a gorgeous suite on the second floor of the manor, decorated in pale blue and silver with a lovely balcony and luxurious en suite bathroom.

Part of her mental preparation for this weekend had been to promise herself she would not think about her career or family—the gaping holes inside of her threatening to tear her apart. Instead, she had been plunged right into the center of the world she was trying to avoid just as she was slated to put on a performance of adoring fiancée in front of Alejandro's closest friends.

How was she supposed to do that with a horse show going on under her nose?

She walked to the window and took in the sprawling English countryside. Even now she could see them setting up the show course in the distance, the lush surrounding forestland providing spectacular scenery.

"This is for you."

She turned to find Alejandro holding out a cream-embossed envelope. Swallowing back the jagged edge inside of her, she crossed to him, took the envelope and tore it open, reading her hostess's sophisticated script.

Cecily,
I hope you will join me in the Rose Room for break-
fast at eight tomorrow morning. I've invited Sadie
and Calli. I'd like to take this opportunity to get to
know all of you better.
Monika

Alejandro peered over her shoulder. "That's nice. You'll like Monika."

She nodded. "I should have a bath so we aren't late."

She attempted to collect herself while immersed in lemon-scented bubbles up to her chin in the luxurious marble tub. Her interaction with Alejandro on the plane wasn't helping.

He had been a rock in the center of the storm this past couple of weeks, there for her in every way. Sensing how disoriented she was, he'd given her carte blanche on her dream stables and worked side by side with her on the plans, an attempt she knew, to distract her, but one that had also thrown her into confusion.

She'd gotten to know him over those quiet dinners they'd shared talking and working through the plans. Had been able to see beneath some of those complex layers of his. Yes, he was tough and ruthless when it came to ac-quiring what he wanted, but she'd also seen more than a few glimpses of the man she'd met in Kentucky—the bru-tally honest, empathetic side of him with the strength of character she'd gravitated to. Leaned on.

If, as she was starting to believe, he *was* that man she'd met, why then was it so hard to take that next baby step in trusting him? Was she so afraid of being wrong again about someone after what Davis had done to her she didn't trust her own judgment anymore, a fear Alejandro's deception had exacerbated? Because she knew she couldn't afford to be wrong in the decisions she was making right now with her life disintegrating around her?

Or was she more afraid of what it would mean if Alejandro *was* that man she'd thought he was? How powerfully drawn she was to him. That she could easily lose her head over him all over again, the one thing she could never do in this convenient arrangement of theirs.

She knew the next step was hers. She simply had no idea what to do.

She felt frozen. *Paralyzed.* Utterly unsure of how to proceed.

Cecily was too quiet. Alejandro had heard enough *I'm fines* uttered by females who were anything but in his lifetime to know she wasn't fine. But she wouldn't tell him what was wrong. He assumed it was the horse show on top of today's announcement, but *who knew?* The guesswork was making him crazy.

He gave her some space as he took a shower and dressed in trousers and a pale blue shirt in deference to the evening's casual attire. Space was what he needed when he was off balance. Maybe that's what Cecily needed too.

Heading to the sitting room just as the clock struck seven, he stopped in his tracks at the sight of his fiancée, dressed and ready to go.

The sapphire silk dress finished far too high on her thighs in his opinion, a pair of sky-high silver stilettos setting off her toned, magnificent legs. There was only one thing a man wanted to do with a dress like that and you couldn't do it in public.

She murmured something about being late. He tore his gaze away from her legs and found his shoes.

"You're stiff as a board," he said as he laced his fingers

through hers and they walked down the massive, center staircase to the mezzanine.

"Not to worry," she said stiffly. "I won't disappoint you. I'm channeling madly in love as we speak."

A slow curl of heat unraveled inside of him. He shouldn't engage—he should keep this thing sane between them—but he was too annoyed to heed his own advice.

He pulled her to a halt in the hallway that led to the terrace, just before they stepped outside. Resting a palm against the wall, he eyed her. "What's wrong?"

A tilt of her chin. "Nothing."

He *hated* that calm, even tone of voice. "Is it the show tomorrow? Today's news?"

"I'll deal with that."

"Then *what is it?*"

"Nothing." She stared at him. "What's the matter with *you*? You've been a bear all afternoon. You keep impressing on me how important tonight is, how much these friendships mean to you, then when I try and focus and be what you need me to be, you look annoyed."

"I *am* annoyed," he growled. "You're driving me crazy."

Her eyes widened. He stepped closer, the first time he'd allowed himself anywhere near her in weeks. Noted the fine lines of strain bracketing her mouth, the wary cast to those blue eyes. "If you are stressed," he murmured, "you need to talk to me. You *used* to talk to me. Why can't you do that?"

A flicker in those blue eyes. "I—I don't know."

He shook his head. "This isn't going to work unless you let me in. Unless you start trusting me."

Confusion, indecision, wrote itself across her face. "I'm trying. Alejandro, I—"

A thread inside him snapped. He took the last step between them, flattened his palm against the wall. Color rode her high cheekbones, her pupils dilating. "What are you doing?"

He cupped her jaw in his fingers and lowered his head to hers, their breath mixing in a seductive, heady heat. "Solving this impasse."

She didn't move away. He considered that progress. Slanting his mouth over hers, he took her lips in a leisurely, persuasive possession designed to melt those icy defenses. She didn't move for a moment, frozen it seemed, then a sigh tore itself from her throat as she relaxed beneath his hands. Soft and pliant beneath his, her mouth was heaven. Her response—that particularly rare combination of innocence and passion that had slayed him from the very beginning nearly brought him to his knees.

She moved closer, her soft curves brushing against the length of him. Unable to resist temptation, he curved his fingers around a bare stretch of toned, sexy thigh and pulled her even closer, his teeth catching the tender flesh of her lower lip in his.

Santo Deus, he wanted her. Had wanted her for weeks. Ever since he'd had that first taste.

"I would say 'get a room,'" a low voice intoned behind them, "but since you already have one, perhaps you should use it."

Cecily stepped back so fast, she tripped over her heels. Alejandro wrapped an arm around her waist to steady her, directing a grin at Stavros. Dressed casually in a white shirt and gray pants, an attractive, black-haired woman at his side, his friend's dark eyes were dancing with amusement.

"Then I would not be here to greet your passably handsome face," Alejandro drawled, slapping him on the shoulder. *"Ola."*

Stavros was, in fact, more than passably handsome. *Swoon-worthy* as some women liked to call his surly, dark good looks. Alejandro wasn't a fan of how he turned that charm on his fiancée now—darkening Cecily's cheeks to a deep shade of rose.

And that was new. Considering his good friend a threat. Particularly since Stavros's new wife was standing at his side.

He studied her as his friend introduced them. Calli wasn't his usual type. Stavros dated worldly, vivacious women who matched his colorful personality. Calli was quiet and unassuming. Pretty—yes. A killer figure, absolutely. But what was it about her that had convinced Stavros to take the plunge into marriage?

It claimed his thoughts as they found Antonio and his new wife, Sadie, on the terrace along with their hosts Sebastien and Monika. Antonio he could understand. You find your son, you claim him—much like his own situation with his unborn child. Stavros, however, had *chosen* to marry this woman from the vast array of females he had at his beck and call in what he suspected might be a convenient marriage. *Something* about her must have stood out.

And maybe, he acknowledged, as the four couples sat down for dinner together on the torch-lit terrace, this was just him trying to understand his preoccupation with the woman on his arm. How Cecily had defied his usual rules of detachment from the very beginning.

He watched her carefully over dinner to make sure she was comfortable, but amidst the good conversation and laughter at the table she relaxed and was much more herself. He relaxed then too and made a good study of Antonio and his new wife.

It was clear the Greek was enamored with the elegant English brunette. In fact, if he wasn't mistaken, he thought Antonio might be in love with her their connection was so strong.

He caught Cecily's gaze drifting to the newly married

couple more than once during the evening, a wistful expression in those sapphire eyes. Guilt gnawed at his edges. He cared about her, he knew that, but he could never give her that love she craved. He'd known it from the very beginning—why he'd been content to walk away. He'd buried that knowledge when he'd persuaded her to marry him because she was having his child. Sacrifices were necessary.

He sat back in his chair and swallowed a mouthful of the legendary Tuscan Cabernet Sebastien was serving. His inability to forge open, loving relationships was something he'd long ago acknowledged. Somewhere along the way, he'd flipped a switch inside of himself, one of self-preservation. Love wasn't something he was ever going to expose himself to—as unreliable as it was intransient. It wasn't something he could reverse engineer for Cecily's sake even if he wanted to. He was just going to have to find other ways to give her what she needed.

Guilt pushed aside, he focused, then, on the excellent conversation between old friends and the entertaining night it turned out to be, but the woman at his side continued to claim the lion's share of his attention.

There was a connection between them tonight, an invisible barrier that had fallen with that kiss they'd shared. An *energy* that drew him like a moth to a flame. *That* he told himself, was what was going to sustain them, because he couldn't imagine that chemistry fading anytime soon.

He kept an arm across the back of her chair, fingers toying idly with her silky blonde curls as darkness fell across the English countryside and the torches burned bright into the night.

When dinner finally concluded, the women elected to turn in early given their eight a.m. breakfast with their hostess. Alejandro tucked Cecily into his side for the walk back to their room, a chill permeating the late-night air. She shivered and moved closer. Heat stoked low in his belly. Snooker—a late night ritual with the men—was not what he had in mind.

The suite was cast in shadows when they entered. Alejandro flicked on a lamp, his eyes never leaving his fiancée.

"Can you help me with my dress before you go?" she requested huskily, turning her back to him.

Her delicate scent wrapped itself around him, filling his head. He moved his fingers to the hook at the top of her dress. Tiny, almost invisible, he managed to undo it then slide the zipper slowly down her back. He thought it might be the most exquisite form of self-torture invented as he uncovered inch after inch of perfect creamy skin, right down to the dip at the small of her back, his second favorite spot on a woman.

His body hardened as he remembered that night in Kentucky. How he'd made her come apart with his hands and mouth on that perfect skin. This time, he knew, he wanted her just like that on that bed, his arm beneath her hips, but with his aching body buried inside her instead in an animalistic possession that matched his mood.

He set his mouth to her nape.

"Alejandro—" she murmured, a strangled note to her voice.

He turned her around in his arms, reading the conflicting emotions in her eyes.

"One step at a time," he said softly. "That's how we do this, *querida*."

Indecision wrote itself across her blue gaze. He was leaning down to kiss her when Stavros pounded on the door.

"Ouaou." Wow. "You are in a filthy mood." Stavros gave Alejandro a sideways look as they made their way downstairs to the billiards room. "Doesn't that ring on her fin-

ger mean you get guaranteed sex, because you resorting to hallways is a desperate measure my friend."

"We weren't in the hallway," Alejandro countered. "We were in our bedroom. And I was on the way."

"No you weren't," Stavros said complacently. "I was merely helping you along."

Alejandro scowled at him. "Instead of us talking about your bad timing, why don't you tell me what's going on with this marriage of yours?"

A deceptively innocent look back. "Meaning…?"

"You come back from Greece with a *wife?* How does that happen?"

"The same way you arriving here with a fiancée does." Stavros lifted a shoulder. "I married her for custody of my company. As good a reason as any."

His friend's response was just a bit too casual, a bit too blasé for him to buy it. It was a surefire sign there were things smoldering beneath that dark façade of his. *Did he have feelings for his wife?*

"What about you?" Stavros gave him a pointed look as they hit the marble mezzanine and headed toward the entertainment wing. "*I* need to be married…produce an heir. Antonio has a child. What's *your* excuse for breaking the eleventh commandment?"

"Have you *looked* at her?"

The Greek pursed his lips. "Am I seriously allowed to answer that question?"

"No."

"Just like I thought," Stavros murmured, pushing open the door of the billiards room. "You are in trouble. Deep trouble."

Alejandro could have told him he was wrong. That a couple nights of hot sex, the transformation of his relationship into the rational, civilized union he'd envisioned would cure what ailed him. But the ritual of opening a seventy-year-old bottle of whiskey distracted him as Sebastien made a toast to the three of them winning the bet.

His usual cryptic self, the Englishman acted as if he'd won the wager, making Alejandro even more sure their challenges had never really been about subsisting without their wallets.

Antonio, looking far more introspective than he had earlier, waded in to suggest his had been about finding his son. Sebastien only inclined his head, saying that had been a bonus, but he needed to look deeper than that.

The Italian laughed it off, as did they all because who knew where Sebastien's head was really at? Who *cared* as the evening devolved into a series of bloodthirstily competitive games of snooker.

Deep into the fifth frame, Sebastien stood by Alejandro's side, eyeing the table while Stavros and Antonio refilled their glasses.

"How was Kentucky?"

"Successful." Alejandro lined up a shot in his head. "Your cover was brilliant, *obrigado*. My grandmother will be happy now."

"And your soon-to-be wife?" Sebastien lounged back against the table. "I like her, Alejandro, a lot. She's exactly what you need—a woman strong enough to stand up to you...to *challenge* you." He lifted a brow. "Are you really prepared to detonate your relationship over an ancient feud?"

"I'm working on a solution to that." Alejandro took a sip of his whiskey, tilted his head back to absorb its mellow burn.

"And if you don't find one?"

"I will." He pointed his glass at the Englishman. "Why did you send me to Kentucky? It wasn't about the wallets, I get that."

Sebastien set his dark gray gaze on him. "There's more

to life than proving you are a better man than your father, Alejandro. Justifying your net worth every single second of the day. Sometimes I think you get so caught up in that you forget who *you* are. What you are capable of."

His skin bristled. "I'm not trying to *prove* I'm a better man than my father, *I am*."

"No one would argue that." Stavros inserted himself into the conversation as he and Antonio returned with their drinks. "Far too serious a topic," he reprimanded Sebastien. "I leave for five minutes and look what happens. Tonight is about the game."

Alejandro couldn't disagree. Stavros had dragged him away from his room at the worst possible moment. He was damn well winning this match.

He did. His luck, however, had run out when he clambered up the stairs in the early hours of the morning to find Cecily, her silky blonde hair splayed across the pillow, curves plastered into a tantalizing piece of cream silk, fast asleep.

CHAPTER NINE

ALEJANDRO WAS UNCHARACTERISTICALLY still asleep when Cecily woke the next morning for her breakfast with the ladies. Still singed from their encounter of the night before, she averted her eyes from all the toned, olive-skinned muscle exposed right down to where the sheet cut across her fiancé's lean hips and pointed herself in the direction of the bathroom instead.

That would not help her composure, something she needed today. The pretty rose-colored dress she slipped on *would*. She did her hair and applied a light coat of make-up, then left Alejandro to sleep and descended the intricate, hand-carved, dark wood staircase to the main floor of the manor.

Besieged by the sights and sounds of today's festivities, her new-found composure was rattled before she'd even reached the bottom step. Horse caravans emblazoned with the rider's names were arriving in the yard, sound systems crackled as they were tested and caterers flitted throughout the house, preparing for the lunch Monika and Sebastien were hosting for the riders and dignitaries—a lunch she and Alejandro had been asked to attend.

Event day buzz had always energized and excited her. Today it tightened her stomach into a ball that refused to unwind. It felt as if the world, *her* world and everything in it was passing her by and there was nothing she could do about it. She wanted to be out there walking the course, thinking through strategy, chatting with her fellow riders. Instead she would merely be a spectator.

Determined to master the day in spite of its wobbly start, she pasted a smile on her face and entered the Rose

Room. She was the last to arrive, Calli looking lovely in a floral print dress while Sadie was elegant in yet another print that hugged her slender curves.

Never the best at these feminine gatherings, she was happy to play with a piece of toast she didn't really want and drink her tea while Calli regaled the table with an amusing tale of Stavros ending up in the pool the night before recovering a priceless bottle of sauterne Sebastien had tossed in.

Monika laughed softly. "That's the sort of thing they do. They thrive on challenging each other. Of course, this most recent challenge takes the cake."

That was when Cecily realized it wasn't just Alejandro who had been undercover. So had Antonio, posing as a mechanic in the garage where Sadie had worked and Stavros, dispatched as a pool boy to the villa in which Calli had lived. The assignment, Monika reported, clearly assuming they'd known all about it, had ostensibly been for the men to go two weeks without their wallets, but Sebastien's wife seemed sure there had been a deeper meaning to each of the individual challenges.

To ruin her family. Cecily set her cup down with a rattle. *This had all started as a game?* She was too dumbfounded to speak. Guessing from the looks on the other women's faces, she wasn't alone.

"What were the stakes in the bet?" she asked Monika.

"If Sebastien won, the men would give up one of their most prized possessions. Alejandro's private island, for instance. If Sebastien lost, he promised to donate half his fortune to charity."

"And all three men completed their challenges?"

Monika nodded. "Sebastien will be making the announcement of the donation in a few weeks' time. He plans to set up a global search and rescue team with it, something that's close to his heart given his near miss last year."

Cecily's head spun as Monika told the story of how Stavros, Antonio and Alejandro had dug Sebastien out of an avalanche. It was a gut-wrenching story, a noble endeavor Sebastien was embarking on, to be sure, but her brain was still caught up in the wager that had brought Alejandro to Esmerelda.

She was trying so hard to get past what he'd done, how he'd deceived her. Had just begun to trust him, *them,* again. But to find out this had been part of a silly bet as her life fell apart at the seams? It made her head want to explode.

Alejandro eyed his fiancée over lunch on the terrace. She looked like some kind of pink confection in the dainty little dress, one he wanted to consume inch by inch. The smoke coming out of her ears, however, suggested the idea of a trip back to their room might not be well received.

Biting back his impatience, he bent his head to hers, keeping his voice low given the dignitaries at their table. "I know that look. What are you so angry about?"

"Your bet came up as a topic of conversation over breakfast."

Ah. He took his sunglasses off. Eyed her. "I didn't tell you about it because it only complicated an already complex situation."

"You don't say." Her eyes flashed a brilliant blue fire. "Do you know how blindsided the three of us were? I felt like a fool."

He rubbed a hand against his pounding temple, the after effects of the whiskey lingering. "I should have told you. But it changes nothing about us Cecily—everything I've told you is the truth."

"The truth," she derided, "is a subjective state of being for you, Alejandro."

Heat seared his belly. "It was an *omission*," he said curtly, "not a mistruth."

"It was *juvenile*, ill thought-out and ill advised. Although Monika," she added, voice dripping with sarcasm, "was quick to point out there was some deeper lesson you were all supposed to be learning. What was yours…*revenge is sweet?*"

"Maybe it was that *you* are sweet, angel, as I seem to have acquired a high-maintenance fiancée along the way."

She made a sound at the back of her throat. Fixed her gaze on his. "And to *think* I was considering being intimate with you again. *Trusting you*, when life is just a joke to you."

"I assure you," he returned in a dangerously low voice, "I take all of this very seriously. I've done nothing *but* since our impetuous night in bed together landed us in this unfortunate…*situation*. It was an expensive move for both of us, *querida*, and the costs keep rising."

Her sapphire eyes snapped with fury. She put her nose in the air and began a conversation with a judge sitting across the table. He slid his sunglasses back on, muttering a curse beneath his breath. No way was he letting her derail them again—destroy what they'd begun building. *This* was ending *now*.

He laced his fingers through hers as they left the lunch and headed for the show jumping ring to watch Natalia ride in her junior class. Cecily tugged on his hand. "We don't need to be joined at the hip."

"Yes we do," he replied evenly. "There are photographers everywhere. Now is not the time to regret your impulsive behavior, *meu carinho*."

Her chin came up. "And I expect you do?"

"In this moment, *sí*." He flashed her a blinding smile as a photographer pointed a camera at them.

Her smile slipped as Natalia bounded up to them, wearing cream colored breeches and a red riding jacket. "Will you walk the course with me?" she asked Cecily, breathlessly. "I always get so nervous before a class I want to upend my stomach."

His fiancée dropped his hand and gave him a victorious look. "Sure. Jump on Sappho and show me her stride."

Cecily walked the course with Natalia, focusing on the technical aspect of the test ahead of the young rider rather than the familiar, almost ritualistic routine she would have done anything to be a part of. She'd thought she might feel better contributing. Instead she felt more ragged inside with every step she took. More *undone*.

When was it going to stop hurting so much? Because right now it felt like never.

She managed to avoid the familiar faces she came across, including Virginia Nelissen, her arch rival on the Dutch team who was competing in a later class. Slipping out of the ring after wishing Natalia good luck, she went to watch in the VIP area with Alejandro and the rest of their group.

The strategy she and Natalia had devised paid off. Cutting the corner at precisely the right angle, Natalia turned in a clear round with a very fast time and placed second in her class. Sebastien, radiating with pride, insisted they all join him and Monika for a celebratory drink in the tent he'd had erected for refreshments.

It was über-hot in there, with the soaring afternoon temperatures, far too many people packed inside far too small a space. Cecily's head throbbed, a band of tension encircling her skull. She really should have eaten more today but her stomach had been so off.

She would find Natalia, congratulate her and leave. But that, of course, proved impossible. She and Alejandro got caught up in an endless round of chit chat with her old social set. Wrapping herself in an impenetrable shield, she allowed nothing and no one to permeate it, including her fiancé she was still furious with.

She was discussing the course with a jubilant Natalia, intent on extracting herself imminently, when Virginia Nelissen tracked her down.

"Cecily." The current number six rider in the world enveloped her in a cloud of perfume and air kisses, causing Natalia to melt away into the crowd. "How did I not know you were going to be here?"

"I'm not riding."

"Why ever not?' Virginia, the circuit's biggest gossip, gave her a speculative look. "It's a fabulous course."

"I'm taking a break," Cecily said woodenly. "That's all."

"Oh," said the Dutch rider, hazel eyes wide with feigned innocence, "I was worried the rumors were true."

Don't bite, don't do it, Cecily. She's poison. But she couldn't help herself.

"What rumors?"

"I heard the powers that be on the American committee were worried you'd lost your edge after the accident. That they didn't think you were a good bet for the team." Virginia lifted a shoulder. "I'm sure it isn't true."

Or was it? Her stomach twisted as she remembered the closed-off conversation she'd had with the team chief. *Did they think she was damaged goods?* Was her career on the rocks? Once you had a reputation for being a broken rider, it tended to stick.

Alejandro joined the two of them. She gave him a frozen look, remaining stiff under the arm he wrapped around her waist, the thick air in the tent closing in around her with every minute that passed.

Confused, shattered, the heat pressing down on her lungs, it was all she could do to function on auto-pilot until Alejandro excused them and pulled her aside.

"This whole routine is getting old," he murmured in her

ear. "You freezing me out, me trying to make this work. It was a bet, Cecily. Get over it."

Perspiration broke out on her brow. She swallowed hard as a wave of nausea rolled over her, noticing the curious looks Sadie and Antonio were directing their way. "Can we get out of here?" she asked sharply, biting back the bile that climbed her throat. "Your friends are watching us."

"When we're finished here." His ebony eyes blazed with heat. "You *know* you can trust me. I'm not going to let you derail us again, just when we're finally getting somewhere."

A cold sweat enveloped her, a clammy film covering her skin. She dragged in a breath, but the air felt too thick, too heavy to speak.

"Cecily." Alejandro's voice sharpened. "What's wrong?"

Darkness swirled around her, everything dissolving into a thick, gray fog. She swayed into him. "I—I can't breathe."

Alejandro cursed and slid an arm around Cecily's waist. He couldn't even see the exit through the crush of people. A glance back at her ash-colored face made his heart pound.

Sinking his fingers into her waist, he hoisted her slight frame into his arms, and elbowed his way through the crowd. Shock guests gaped at them. Alejandro threw a laconic smile in Antonio's direction. "Lovers quarrel," he said loudly enough that everyone in the immediate vicinity could hear. "Only one way to solve this problem."

The crowd parted like the Red Sea. A blast of fresh air hit him as soon as he walked outside, making him realize how oppressively hot it had been in there for his *pregnant fiancée*. Furious at himself for being so insensitive, he carried Cecily up the hill and into the house. He didn't stop until they were inside the cool, quiet confines of their suite, away from prying eyes.

He set her down on the edge of the bed and made her put her head between her knees. "Breathe," he instructed, sitting down beside her. She took a deep breath, then another. He made her continue until she was taking regular, even inhales of air.

"I can't believe you did that," she said when she sat up, still pale but far less gray.

"Would you have preferred I let you pass out in front of everyone?"

"No." Her chin dropped. "But what are they going to think?"

"That we are having sex." He was amused to see that brought her full color back. "Why on earth didn't you tell me how you were feeling?"

"I thought it would pass. It usually does...but it was so hot in there. And," she admitted, eyes on his, "I was angry with you."

His gaze darkened. He stood, walked to the sideboard and poured a glass of water from the crystal jug. Carrying it back to the bed, he handed it to her and sat down.

She took a sip of the water. Exhaled with a deep sigh. "I told myself I was going to be tough today—prove I can get through this."

"You were tough. You walked that course with Natalia. You faced what must have been a difficult day head-on."

She shook her head. "I let Virginia get to me. She told me she'd heard a rumor—that the selection committee might not have picked me for the team. It...upset me."

"You can't listen to that kind of conjecture," he reprimanded. "She's playing with your head, Cecily. You of all people know how cut throat the competition is."

"But she's connected. What if it's the truth?"

"If it is, there's nothing you can do about it except prove them wrong. Focus on what you *can* affect rather than what you can't." He arched a brow at her. "Remember what we talked about in Kentucky? *You* are the master of your own destiny. No one else."

"That's just it," she said quietly, "I can't *prove* anything right now. I'm scared of what this year off—this baby—is going to do to my career."

His heart tugged at her vulnerability. "Your mother had you when she was young and remained highly competitive. You will do the same because you are just as fiercely competitive. You are a *Hargrove.*"

A hint of her trademark stubborn defiance crept back into her blue gaze. "Use the year to get your stables up and running," he advised. "Find another couple of horses to back up Bacchus and Derringer so when you come back, you come back even stronger than before. That's what winners do. They build on their setbacks. They use them to make them stronger."

She eyed him. "Why do you always know exactly the right thing to say?"

"Because I know what it's like to be on top. What it's like to be surrounded by people whose mission in life is to tear you down. Protect yourself by having an unshakeable vision. Don't give the Virginias of the world the opportunity to steal your joy."

Her gaze darkened. She looked down at the glass she held balanced on her lap, the afternoon sun arcing off its finely cut crystal edges. "You asked me once who I was doing this for. I thought about it a lot after you left. I know now it's for me. Of course it's for my mother too," she acknowledged, "but this dream, the dream to be the best that I have, comes from *me*, not from what I'm *expected* to be. Riding is who I am, Alejandro. It's what I love. I can't imagine doing anything else."

"Then tune out the noise," he said softly. "Follow your heart."

She nodded. A play of emotion moved through those

beautiful eyes. "What you said about trust… I have trouble trusting because of what happened with a previous relationship of mine. I was engaged to a man named Davis Hampden Randolph when I was twenty-three—of the banking Randolphs. My father does business with him."

He tipped a brow. "An arranged match?"

She shook her head. "I was mad about Davis. I was about to marry him and move to Savannah when I found out weeks before the wedding he was mad about his mistress too—he just wasn't going to marry her."

Shades of his father. "I'm sorry," he said quietly. "That must have been difficult."

A shadow whispered across her gaze. "I was a political choice for him. Funnily enough, when I gave him the ring back, it turned out I was the last to know."

His stomach hollowed out. He knew that humiliation. Had watched his mother go through it more times than he could count. And he, *he* had not made the situation any better by deceiving Cecily, then walking away.

He curled his fingers around hers. "I promise I will never hurt you like that. You will get honesty from me but never pain."

Her chin dropped. "Every time I've invested myself in someone in my life I've gotten hurt, Alejandro. Melly, Davis, losing my mother, my *father's* lack of caring…" She shook her head. "I know this is a practical thing between us—exactly as I was for Davis. That we are doing this for our child. But I need to know if I put my trust in you, that trust is inviolate. That *you* are willing to invest in us too."

He almost laughed at the unnecessary nature of the request. He'd been invested in her from the beginning—far more than he ever should have been. He thought it might be that extreme vulnerability of hers—how it tapped into a part of him that remembered all too vividly what it felt like to be at the mercy of the world. To have those who should have protected you fail in their promises.

It made him wonder about Sebastien's analysis of him. If perhaps he was capable of more with Cecily because he did care about her. Maybe *that*, he ventured, was what he could offer her beyond the love he couldn't give her. He could be the one person who never let her down. Who taught her she was worthy of that promise.

He set his gaze on her. "I *am* invested," he said quietly. "I've always been invested. I proposed marriage between us because I thought it could work, because we are good together. Because you have many of the qualities I admire in a woman, not just because you are having my baby. But *you* need to believe it can work too, Cecily. You need to trust me again."

She nodded. "I'm learning to. But there's only so many of these landmines I can take and still do that, Alejandro." She arced a brow at him. "Is there anything else I should know? Because you should tell me *now* and not later."

"Yes," he said silkily, running a finger down her cheek. "I have a date with Antonio at the shooting range in twenty minutes. Which means *you* have time to rest up for our date tonight and find a sexy dress to wear, because *we*," he added deliberately, "are picking up where we left off last night, *querida*. No distractions, no manufactured dramas and no interruptions."

Her eyes widened. He lowered his mouth to hers, giving in to the lush temptation in front of him. "And if Stavros comes knocking," he murmured against her lips, "I swear I will kill him with my bare hands."

CHAPTER TEN

CECILY HAD NEVER been so nervous in her entire life. She had changed her dress three times while Alejandro had showered and shaved after his shooting date with Antonio and still she wasn't convinced she'd made the right choice.

Champagne with a definite hint of pink, the sultry dress hugged her body like a glove, plunging at the neckline to show off the curves of her breasts, dipping in to highlight her tiny waist then flaring out over the full line of her hips. Very Marilyn Monroe, she'd thought as she'd purchased it on Madison Avenue last week. Sexy as Alejandro had requested. But was it too much?

"Oh, no," murmured Calli as they stood under the elegant marquee set up on the Waldenbrook grounds. "You look like an angel. A very *wicked* angel. Alejandro can't pick his tongue up off the ground."

Her gaze slid to her fiancé who stood speaking with Sebastien and Antonio. He looked gorgeously sophisticated and untouchable in a black tuxedo, dark hair slicked back from his face. As far removed from the man she'd met in Kentucky as it was possible to be. And yet tonight she was sure she knew him. That she'd always known him. What was terrifying was what that meant.

The night she'd spent with Alejandro in his cabin had been a forbidden assignation with no consequences attached to it. Tonight there were so many consequences involved her stomach was doing backflips.

She was about to place herself in the hands of a man she hoped wouldn't shatter the last piece of heart she had left. To fully trust him as she hadn't yet let herself do because she needed to in order to make this marriage work. For the child they were going to have.

That didn't mean it wasn't terrifying. Because it was. Keeping that level head she'd promised herself was going to be key, banishing those feelings she still harbored for him to restricted territory, except keeping a level head was almost impossible to do as the man in question executed a subtle seduction over dinner in the beautifully set up marquee.

Seated with Stavros, Calli, Antonio and Sadie at one of the round tables dressed with white linen, candles and fresh roses, it was all she could do to keep her mind on the conversation with Alejandro's eyes and hands on her the entire evening in an orchestrated campaign meant to drive her mad.

Her composure was in shreds by the time they got up to dance, Sebastien and Monika kicking things off. The Englishman and his wife had eyes only for each other, the deep love they shared patently obvious. It led to dangerous thinking on Cecily's part. If Sebastien, once a confirmed bachelor, as steadfastly opposed to marriage as Alejandro had once been according to Monika, could change so much with the right woman, perhaps Alejandro could too?

And that, she castigated herself as Alejandro took her hand and led her onto the dance floor to join Sebastien and Monika, was the kind of thinking she needed to avoid if she was going to survive this relationship.

Heart hammering in her breast, pulse beating so fast she felt like she was in a drag race, she allowed him to pull her close, his fingers wrapped around hers, her head tucked beneath his chin.

Their fit was so perfect, so right, it sent her spiraling back to that night in Kentucky when he'd held her beneath the stars. When she'd given up fighting the attraction between them because it was simply too powerful to resist.

His heart beat a steady, staccato rhythm beneath her ear. A sigh left her lips.

Alejandro drew back, his gorgeous, inky black eyes glittering with amusement. "Are you all right, *querida*?"

"Fully recovered," she murmured, "from this afternoon at least. This campaign you are waging has me distinctly on edge."

The grooves on either side of his mouth deepened. "You seduced me last time. Surely turnabout is fair play?"

"*I* seduced *you*...the operative words. I knew what I was doing then."

"And now?"

"Now I have no idea what I'm doing."

"Yes you do," he said softly. "You know this is right. Why so nervous, angel?"

"Because," she whispered, so caught up in him she was a lost cause, "it was...*magical*."

His gaze darkened. Tightening his arm around her waist, he brought his mouth to her ear, his stubble rasping the sensitive skin of her cheek. "I will make it magical. *Trust me*."

She melted, her insides dissolving into liquid honey. He pressed a kiss to the sensitive spot behind her ear, sending a shiver through her. She arched her neck to give him better access, tiny bolts of electricity exploding across her skin as he tasted her with an open-mouthed caress.

"Oh," she said, jolted out of her reverie. "That's odd."

"What?"

"Sadie just walked off the dance floor."

He straightened, his gaze flicking to Antonio who stood at the side of the dance floor, looking a little dazed. "That is odd."

She watched Sadie hurry toward the house, her heels sinking into the grass. She stopped, removed her shoes, then ran the rest of the way, stilettos hanging from her fingers. *As if she couldn't move fast enough.*

"Should I go after her do you think?"

"No." The curtness of Alejandro's tone claimed her attention. The banked fire in his eyes held it. "No distractions, no drama and no interruptions," he said meaningfully. "Let them handle it."

Her stomach curled. When the song ended, her fiancé had a quick word with Sebastien and Monika, wrapped his arm around her waist and walked her across the lawn toward the house. Her heels kept sinking into the grass just as Sadie's had. Pulling to a halt, she bent and tugged them off.

Alejandro increased his pace, Cecily half running to keep up with him. When they reached the cobblestoned walkway he swung her up into his arms and carried her up a set of back stairs she hadn't even known existed.

"Could be glass," he said blithely.

"You just like carrying me," she teased.

"Yes," he agreed, "I do. And it gets us there faster."

She clung to him as he walked down the hallway toward their suite. Outside their room, he paused and shifted her weight to open the door. She wrapped her arms around his neck, bringing his mouth down to hers for a kiss. The hot, open-mouthed caress was wild and delicious, sizzling the blood in her veins.

Muttering an oath, he broke the kiss. She made a sound of protest, twining her fingers tighter into his hair. He ignored her, turning the handle and carrying her inside.

His eyes were like burning coal as he set her down. "Stavros already thinks I'm out of control when it comes to you."

"And are you?" she asked archly.

"Not yet," he murmured, walking her backward until she collided with the hard surface of the wall. "We are, after all, on the other side of the door. But there's still time yet."

Oh, my. Her shoes clattered to the floor as he buried his fingers in her hair and kissed her—slow, drugging caresses that made her sag weakly against the plaster. *Good Lord the man knew how to kiss. How had she even resisted this?*

Lost in him, in the wild scent of pure, aroused male, she obeyed when he nudged her legs apart and stepped between them. Heat in the air, so thick she could taste it, she gasped as he settled his hips against hers, imprinting her with a hot, hard masculine demand she could feel right through the fabric of his trousers.

"Alejandro," she whispered.

Palming her thigh, he pressed his thumb to the hollow where hip met leg and spread her wider apart. She flattened her palms against the wall as he thrust against her with a slow, erotic focus that stole her breath.

Dark, sensual eyes met luminous blue. "You want me, angel? I want to hear you say it."

Her tongue seemed glued to the roof of her mouth. He moved closer, resting his hands on the wall on either side of her, letting her feel every hard, pulsing inch of him.

"You're punishing me," she breathed.

"*Sim,*" he agreed. "I can't focus. I can't think anymore for wanting you. So say the words, *querida. End this.*"

She closed her eyes. Rested her forehead against his chest, bones too weak to hold her. "Make love to me, Alejandro," she whispered. "I want your hands all over me."

He picked her up and carried her to the massive, king-sized bed with a speed that made her dizzy. Sitting down with her on his lap, he ran his thumb over her trembling bottom lip before he took possession, his kiss a shimmering, sensual meeting of the mouths that promised only exquisite pleasure.

Her skin felt cool as he slipped the straps of her dress

from her shoulders and pushed it down to her waist. Bare under his gaze, body vibrating with tension, she felt her nipples harden in blatant invitation. The lust in his eyes as he drank her in coiled her insides tight. Her heart slammed in her chest as he bent her back over his arm and sampled one rosy tip, then the other, the erotic flick of his tongue, the hard suction of his mouth driving her wild.

She moved restlessly beneath him. Lifting his mouth from her flesh, he set her on the bed, stretched her out like a feast for his consumption. Her eyes were glued to his as he placed a warm hand on her thigh, pushed her dress up to her waist.

"Alejandro."

"Shh." His big palm scaled the taut, trembling skin of her abdomen. "We're both wound up. I'm going to give you some relief first, *meu carinho*. Make you feel good. If I take you now, it won't be good for you."

She could almost guarantee it would be, but she wasn't about to argue when he sank his fingers into the sides of her panties and stripped them off. Her teeth dug into her lip, palms went damp as he pushed her thighs apart with gentle hands and settled himself in between them.

She tensed as he slid his palms beneath her hips to lift her up.

"Let me," he murmured, breath hot against her most intimate flesh.

And then there was only the delicate slide of his tongue against her overheated, aching body. Light so light, it was just enough to tease, to make her crazy. She arched into his touch, a desperate plea on her tongue. Deeper he delved, his sensual, leisurely enjoyment of her as he stroked and tasted her making it clear he loved to do this to her.

It turned her on to watch. Made her crazy. She cried out when he closed his mouth over her sensitized flesh and sucked gently. Shoved a fist in her mouth as she absorbed the waves of pleasure that rolled over her. Slow and languorous at first, they gathered in intensity as he consumed every centimeter of her as if he couldn't get enough.

She begged him hoarsely for relief. He captured her swollen nub between his teeth; razed her sensitive flesh. A flash of white lightning chased through her, fleeting, *almost there*. And then his mouth was back, the delicious lap of his tongue speeding up in intensity and she tipped over the edge, falling headlong into a shimmering river of pleasure so intense it locked her spine.

Alejandro moved up Cecily's beautiful body, nuzzling her damp, velvety skin, absorbing the tremors that racked her limbs. He was shaking, so into her reactions he was hovering on the razor's edge.

Leaving her bathed in the aftershocks, he rolled off the bed, stripped off his clothes and slid on a condom, his flesh so sensitized, so swollen, he had to grit his teeth to do it. Cecily watched him from the bed, looking so sexy and disheveled, half-clad in the golden dress, having been thoroughly consumed by him, he was tempted to take her like that. *Like a fallen angel*.

But he wanted her naked more—all of her lush curves bare beneath his hands. And he knew exactly *how* he wanted to take her because he'd been dreaming about it for weeks.

Stepping back to the bed, he wrapped his fingers around hers, drew her up onto her knees and unzipped the back of her dress. Sliding it over her head, he exposed her delectable, hour glass figure.

His eyes held hers. "I want you on your hands and knees," he murmured. "Can I have you like that?"

A flush crept into her cheeks, her eyes huge, glittering sapphires against pale honey skin. There was shock there, yes, but also a deep pulsing excitement that pushed his own higher. Dropping a kiss on her shoulder, he placed her on her hands and knees. She was trembling, anticipating his touch as he joined her on the bed, caged her legs between his and found the sexy hollow of her back with his mouth.

She arched into his touch with a low moan. His blood fizzled in his veins. Trailing his hand over the slope of her beautiful bottom, he slid his fingers between her thighs and rubbed at her damp, silken skin with the heel of his hand. A gasp escaped her. He bit down on his lip, leashing the urgent demand of his body as she pushed back against his hand, riding his touch.

He waited until she was wet and more than ready for him before he covered her body with his; rested his throbbing length in the curve of her buttock.

It was hot and erotic to have her like this, utterly at his mercy. Her fractured, shallow breathing said she felt it too.

"Cecily," he murmured, pressing his mouth to her back, "you with me?"

She nodded. He ran his hand up the inside of her thigh and widened her stance. One hand on her hip, he guided the crest of his erection to her slick, wet flesh.

Her breath hitched. "I'll take it so slow," he murmured. "I promise you. Trust me."

Her body was silken and welcoming, wrapping around him like a hot, velvet glove. It took every bit of his experience, his self-control, to move slowly, allowing her body to adjust to his. Finally, he was buried inside her, hips flush with her buttocks. Tipping his head back, he exhaled. She felt impossibly tight, impossibly good—like heaven on earth.

"Alejandro," she murmured, reaching a hand back to him.

"Shh." He set a palm against her stomach, anchoring her, holding her in place as he stroked deep inside her. It was more intense for her this way, he could feel it in the tension of her body, in the low sounds she made at the back of her throat. Relaxing as her body melted around his, she met his thrusts with an eagerness that threw all his composure out the window. Shredded his self-control.

"Angel," he murmured, flattening his palm against her stomach, feeling the tremors that raked through her. Blood pounded against his temples as he took her hips in a firm grip and stroked into her with hard, soul-shaking thrusts that threw him right to the edge.

When he reached between her legs to take her with him, she made a broken sound. "Alejandro—"

He froze, buried deep inside her.

"I need to see you. *Please.*"

The desire to carry his fantasy to its insanely good conclusion crumbled at the emotion in her voice. Pulling out of her, he picked her up and wrapped her legs around him so they were face to face, his heat buried inside of her in a single, smooth movement that made her gasp.

"Better?"

She dug her nails into his shoulders, beautiful eyes fixed on his, bright and unclouded. "Yes," she breathed.

He had his doubts in that moment he'd ever be able to deny her anything if it meant he could keep those eyes bruise-free, the spell she cast over him was so complete. His need to protect her, to *have* her, had always been far more powerful than his common sense.

He distracted himself with her lush mouth, pushing that far too telling thought from his head. Her mouth against his, his hands under her buttocks, he brought her down on him again and again, the intimacy of their position, the caress of her silky flesh as he slid in and out of her a perfection he couldn't describe.

His head nearly exploded when she reached between her legs to pleasure herself, throwing her head back and giving herself to him unconditionally.

"*Meu Deus*, that is sexy," he murmured, heart stuttering in his chest. Her lashes fluttered down over her cheeks. Heat singed his skin as he watched her stroke herself to the edge. When her silken muscles clenched tight around him, squeezing him in a vise-like grip, he closed his eyes and gave himself to her in a shuddering release that seemed to go on forever.

Her blue eyes were full of questions when he opened his. *Hope. Expectation.* Gathering her in his arms, he avoided them all, murmuring quiet words into her hair until she fell asleep.

Nowhere near possessing the ability to do the same, he spent twenty minutes staring at the wall then slid out of bed, threw on some sweats and walked out onto the terrace with a cold glass of water.

Bathed in the light of a spectacular orange and gold harvest moon, he stared down at the abandoned marquee, flapping in the breeze. Told himself it had just been good sex—perhaps the best of his life. That she was to be the mother of his child—of course he would *feel* something for her. But he knew it for the mistruth that it was. He'd never been able to flip a switch with Cecily like he had with every other woman in his life—to separate his emotions from his lust.

She affected him—no question about it. Watching her walk out there today to help Natalia, into a world she loved, one that was making her bleed inside she missed it so much, had affected him profoundly. Her strength and her courage always had. But allowing himself to bring that emotion into this relationship wasn't something he could afford to do. He would only let himself feel so far, then he would cut it off and Cecily would be the one getting hurt.

He took a long draw of the water, absorbing the cool slide of the liquid down his throat. He'd finally gotten his relationship with Cecily back on track. Now he needed to ensure it became the rational, even keel affair he'd envisioned for the sake of the child they were having. Particularly given what lay ahead.

He'd heard radio silence from Clayton Hargrove, something he'd have to deal with when they got home. He had a feeling with Clayton's supreme arrogance in play this might all get worse before it got better—yet another reason to keep an already complex relationship from going places it could never go.

CHAPTER ELEVEN

"RELAX," ALEJANDRO MURMURED as they stepped off the jet outside of Brussels, deep in the heart of Salazar country. "My grandmother has promised to be on her best behavior."

Cecily gave him a long look. *Relax? She was walking into enemy territory.* About to meet the woman who refused to be in the same room as a Hargrove. How was she supposed to accomplish that?

He slid an arm around her waist and tugged her into his side as they walked across the tarmac toward the jeep that waited, a silver-haired, diminutive figure standing beside it.

Cecily had met Adriana Salazar once when Alejandro's grandmother had presented her with a rosette at a show in Germany. A tiny powerhouse, she'd struck Cecily as having an iron spine. Proud. *Regal.*

All those qualities met her now as they came to a halt in front of the hawk-eyed eighty-three-year-old, La Reve's glorious seventy-five acres spread out behind her like a vibrant green picture postcard.

"You remind me of your mother," were the first words out of the matriarch's mouth as she stepped forward to take Cecily's hands in hers. "You could be twins."

Unsure if that was a compliment or not, Cecily brushed a kiss to both of Adriana's lined cheeks. "Lovely to meet you," she murmured. "We met in Germany of course, but it was very brief."

"Yes," Adriana said. "You had a hell of a ride that day. You are gutsy, just like your mother was."

She chose to take that as a compliment. "Thank you."

Alejandro's grandmother gave her grandson a warm hug, the deep affection between them obvious. "Come," she said, gesturing toward the jeep. "I have lunch waiting."

The lovely meal in the Spanish, hacienda-style house was utterly civilized as Alejandro had promised, only the three of them in attendance with Alejandro's mother, Luisa, off at a show. It was when Adriana took Cecily on a tour of La Reve after the meal, as Alejandro caught up on work, that the more probing questions came.

She was clearly being vetted as Alejandro's choice of bride as they explored the lush Belgian countryside in the jeep. Prepared for it, Cecily answered Adriana's curious, sometimes blunt questions with honest, straightforward answers…and fell in love with La Reve along the way.

The sprawling countryside was magnificent, the architecturally complex indoor schooling rings the work of a master, but it was the stunning, dark wood stables with their cathedral ceilings and beautiful chandeliers that stole her heart.

It was there that Adriana housed her center for equine therapy where horses and riders from around the region came seeking her expert help. It had been in her head ever since Alejandro had helped her heal Bacchus that she might someday provide those same facilities in her own stables. She listened with rapt fascination as Adriana talked about the program, asking question after question.

"You're interested in that type of work," Alejandro's grandmother commented when they finally concluded the tour in the late afternoon with a glass of lemonade on the porch.

Cecily nodded. "Bacchus and I had a bad accident in London. Alejandro helped us to get past it. I'm not sure we would have without him."

An assessing look from those hawk-like eyes. "You care for him."

She nodded. "I had no idea who he was when I met him. I fell for the man with all the trappings stripped away."

Adriana's gaze moved back to the activity in the yard, a young groom leading an impressive black stallion toward the barn. "Alejandro tells me you didn't know about Bacchus's lineage."

"No," she said evenly, "I thought he was descended from Nightshade. That's what I was always told."

Adriana rested her head against the back of the chair, a frown drawing her brows together. "I never understood it."

"Understood what?"

"Why your mother didn't know." She looked over at Cecily. "Luisa and Zara had an argument after the world championships the year your mother won silver. A big blow-out. Luisa lashed out, calling Zara a coward for refusing to admit Zeus was stolen property. Zara said it was all lies."

Cecily shook her head. "My mother *didn't* know."

Adriana lifted a shoulder. "I had no proof. DNA typing wasn't available then. But there was a groom who had worked at the stables where Diablo was studded. We had him ready to testify in a court case—until your father's money got to him."

Her skin stung. "Did Luisa tell my mother about the groom?"

Adriana nodded. "Luisa told her not to be so naïve. She said Zara seemed flattened…that she left after the awards ceremony and never went to the party."

Confusion consumed her. That would have been weeks before her mother died—before that awful argument with her father. But surely her mother would have told her if she'd known? They had never kept secrets from each other—not even the smallest ones. Especially about something like this.

But if that was true, what *had* her parents been arguing about that night?

She shook off the uneasy feeling that ran through her. "I'm sure she didn't know," she said to Adriana.

"Even if she did," reasoned Alejandro as they walked out to the pasture after dinner to enjoy the spectacular sunset, "does it really matter now? Perhaps she was protecting you."

She shook her head. "She would never have done that. We told each other everything. We were building our careers on those horses."

And another lie would destroy her right now. Alejandro laced his fingers through hers as they walked down the cobblestoned path that lined the pastures, voluminous, silver-leafed chestnut trees swaying overhead.

It was a stunning night, the sunset painting streaks of orange, yellow and pink across the sky, the grazing horses silhouetted against the blaze of color. But his fiancée's attention was elsewhere, her face creased with her current preoccupation.

"So what did you think of La Reve?" he asked. "Pretty impressive?"

"Yes." A smile lit her face. "The equine therapy center is amazing. I was blown away by the work they do. I peppered Adriana with so many questions she was likely glad to get rid of me."

"I'm sure that isn't true." He'd watched his grandmother softening up to Cecily all day, no more immune to her charms than he was.

"I was thinking," she said, shooting him a sideways look, "of asking you to teach me what your grandmother taught you so I could offer those services in our stables. It helped Bacchus so much, I think it could do the same with others."

And her. He didn't miss the subtle psychological cue. "It's a big time investment. You will have your career and a new baby to think about."

"I have a year before that happens. We could train the grooms so I have back up when I'm busy."

The sparkle in her eyes was irresistible. She'd clearly been thinking about this. "It's a great idea," he conceded. "But you should ask my grandmother to teach you, not me. And that should wait until we get this issue with your father sorted."

She nodded, a shadow moving across her gaze. He bit down the antagonism that rose inside of him. He was dealing with Clayton Hargrove as soon as they got home.

"Do you think she'd say yes?"

He nodded. "My grandmother has always been a teacher first. It's her great love."

She fell quiet then as they walked in silence to their destination, a lush, green pasture in which a dozen horses grazed.

"It's so gorgeous," Cecily murmured as they stood watching the horses cavort and play before they came in for the night. "I can see why you were so happy here as boys." Her eyes were bright as she looked up at him in the fading light. "There's this air about it here, this *spirit* I can't describe. More like when my mother was alive at Esmerelda."

He nodded. "It comes from my grandmother. She's competitive, she likes to win, but nothing comes before her horses. They are her lifeblood."

Her lashes swept down. "It must have been great therapy for you boys to be here, surrounded by all of this. I can see why your grandmother means so much to you."

"She was the glue," he said simply. "She insisted we come here instead of being exposed to the toxic environment at home. She knew the grounding effect being around the horses would have on us." He rubbed a hand over the stubble on his jaw. "Those first few summers, Joaquim and I were broken. We had no conception of what love was. My grandmother gave it to us. She was the one thing that made sense when nothing else did."

A wet sheen blanketed her eyes, turning them an iridescent blue. "Sometimes that's all you need," she said quietly, "that one person who believes in you—who gives you that unconditional love."

Something unraveled inside of him. *Santo Deus,* she tore him apart.

"Yes," he agreed huskily, "sometimes that's all you need." He pressed a kiss to the top of her head, dangerously close to a host of emotions that were strictly off limits to him.

She pulled back to look up at him. "How do you feel?" she asked. "About our baby?"

The question caught him off guard. He thought about it for a moment, realized his feelings had morphed from shock into something deeper he couldn't describe. "Hopeful," he finally said, "that I can do things differently. That I can give our child all the things I never had…that *we* can give he or she a happy childhood."

Her eyes darkened. "I think you will be a better parent for your experiences, Alejandro. You will *know* what's important for our child because you have been there."

Perhaps. And perhaps he might severely disappoint her with his inability to foster a deep, open relationship with their child, exactly what he couldn't offer her.

"What I do *know,*" he said quietly, shaking it off as he tucked a lock of her hair behind her ear, "is that we are going to do this together. If one of us falters, the other one will pick them up. It will be a team effort."

"Yes," she agreed huskily, "it will be."

He directed her toward the fence with a hand at her

waist. "Would you like to see your engagement present now?"

Her brows pulled together. "I didn't know we were doing that."

"Not officially no." He pulled an apple out of his pocket. Made a clicking sound with his teeth to catch the attention of a striking, chestnut-brown Belgian warm blood grazing a few feet away. The horse lifted his head, saw the apple in his hand and trotted over, tail held high.

They climbed up on the bottom rung of the fence. "This is Socrates," he said as the stallion butted his head playfully against his closed hand, looking for the apple. "I know he's not Bacchus and I *will* get you Bacchus back, but Socrates's lineage is nearly as impressive. He's my grandmother and I's progeny. We think he's going to be a brilliant jumper."

Cecily stared at him, then at the handsome horse with the white blaze down his face. "What are you saying?" she breathed.

"He's yours."

Her eyes widened. "You can't give him to me."

"Why not? You need a back-up horse. I can't think of a better way to cement the ties between our two families. It's the perfect symbolic union."

She bit her lip. "Your grandmother is okay with this?"

"Yes." He handed her the apple. Socrates pursued it, butting Cecily's hand now. She laughed and opened her palm, the stallion burying his muzzle in her hand and disposing of the apple in two big bites.

"Why Socrates?" she asked.

"I'm a football fan. Soccer," he elaborated, "for you. Socrates was a great Brazilian midfielder."

A smile tipped her lips. "Socrates it is, then."

The stallion stayed for a little more attention then wandered away. Cecily climbed off her perch, stood on tiptoe and kissed him.

It was the sweetest, simplest kiss they had ever shared and it drove a stake right through his heart.

Cecily didn't know what to do with her heart on the walk back to the house. It thumped in her chest in the strangest of ways and refused to stop as she and Alejandro climbed the stairs to their suite of rooms that overlooked the lake.

He murmured something about having to work and plopped himself down in front of his computer in the sitting room. She showered and pulled on a filmy blue nightie, her mind still caught up in the very personal, undeniably special gift he'd just given her.

He kept doing these things that melted her heart. Coming on the heels of last night's passionate, explosive encounter between them, it put reckless thoughts in her head. Like maybe they *could* be more, because she was sure he felt something for her.

Or maybe, she conceded, running a brush through her hair in a ruthless stroke, she was just seeing what she wanted to see. If she were smart, she knew, she would ignore this pull between her and her fiancé just as he was doing right now. Give them both time to breathe. But there were too many questions raging through her head for her to think straight.

Had her mother known about Zeus? What had her parents been arguing about the morning she'd died?

A vice gripped her chest. She couldn't stand for one more thing to not be as it seemed...for one more piece of her life to come careening apart, because her memories of her mother were all she had.

She tried to tell herself how fragile she was. How much Alejandro was coming to mean to her. How *dangerous* that was to her. But right now he seemed like the only real thing in a sea of uncertainty. Nothing could seem to stop her feet from moving as she put down the brush and walked into the sitting room where he was working.

To hell with the consequences.

Slipping behind him on the sofa, she ran her hands up the taut, muscular skin of his back. The heat, the masculinity of him, singed her fingertips beneath the well-worn material of his T-shirt. Sent her pulse racing.

She set her mouth to his nape.

A tremor ran through him. "Cecily—"

She trailed open-mouthed, sensual kisses over the hot, salty skin exposed by the neck of his shirt. Slid her arms around his waist, imprinted her breasts against the muscled skin she'd just been touching. "You sure you want to work?"

"I need to get this report finished before—"

She dropped her hand to the hard length of him beneath his jeans. A curse left his mouth. He was steel beneath the denim, sizzling her blood in her veins.

Suddenly she was upside down, thrown over his shoulder, Alejandro heading toward the bedroom before she had a chance to breathe. And then it was her battling to regain her equilibrium as he deposited her on the bed, took her mouth in a series of hot, hungry kisses in between which he ripped off his jeans and pulled his T-shirt over his head.

"You are killing me," he murmured, eyes holding hers in a suspended, searing moment she felt all the way to her toes, "slowly but surely."

She sucked in a breath as he rode her nightie up her body with his hands and pulled it over her head. *This* was an Alejandro she didn't know, the intensity in him bubbling over the edges, seeping into her skin.

She felt the burn of his gaze on her bare skin seconds before he pushed her back on the bed and braced himself on his elbows above her, a solid wall of sheer male power that made her mouth go dry.

He ran a possessive hand down her body, lingering on the dips and curves he found. Her pulse stuttered, then took off at a dead run. This wasn't going to be a languid, leisurely seduction. It was going to be something else entirely.

Cupping her breasts, he traced his fingertips over the velvety points. Rolled the sensitive peaks between thumb and forefinger until she moaned and moved restlessly beneath him. Satisfying her demand, he palmed the curve of her belly with his hand, then drew his fingers down over the sensitive crease of her thigh.

She opened instinctively for him, eyes on his as he slid a hard male thigh between hers, moving against her in a sensual, breathtaking rhythm. She reached up, curled a hand around his nape and brought his mouth down to hers for an intensely erotic, open-mouthed kiss.

The friction achingly good, her body beyond ready for him, a low plea left her lips. Releasing her mouth, he slid a hand beneath her head to fist in her hair, sliding his other hand down her leg to urge her thigh up and over his hip. With a single, hard thrust he was buried inside of her, her breath escaping on a harsh gasp.

He kissed her through the slow, deep ride he took her on, stroking into her body with deliberate, sweet slides until her insides were a hot shimmer and all she could feel was him. Every inch of her catching fire, she shattered apart, nails digging into his biceps. He came with her, his powerful body swelling, expanding, spilling his scalding heat inside her.

She'd never been so lost and found all in one moment. So sure she'd made an irrevocable choice she could never take back.

CHAPTER TWELVE

ALEJANDRO PACED THE floor of his lower Manhattan office the morning after his and Cecily's return from Belgium, managing the delicate threads of the Columbian acquisition while simultaneously castigating himself for allowing his relationship with Cecily to devolve into the emotional affair it had become.

Clearly he couldn't be trusted not to sink into that realm with her, which necessitated a cooling off period while he figured out how to handle his vulnerable, irresistible fiancée. Because that couldn't happen again between them— another of those charged encounters guaranteed to push their relationship off the track.

His conference call droned on, digressing into legalese he couldn't be bothered to follow. Stopping in front of the windows, he braced his palms on the sill and took in a gray, stormy-looking view of the Hudson. Most people would welcome that level of emotion in their relationship, he acknowledged. For him it was a place he would never go because he knew where it led.

No matter how good he and Cecily were together, no relationship retained that shiny, newly purchased glow. Whether boredom, friction or simply like turning to dislike, all good things came to an end. He'd watched his parents reenact that vicious pattern over and over again and it never ended well, passion and happiness turning to anger, then to hatred and back again until he'd been begging for them to end it. It wasn't something he'd ever subject himself or his child to. Nor would he raise Cecily's expectations as to the type of relationship he could provide.

Better to take his own advice and focus on the things

he could affect such as attacking the root cause of all of his problems.

His conference call mercifully came to an end. Discarding his headset, he sat down at his desk and messaged his lawyer.

Is the letter ready?

Just finished. Want me to bring it over?

Please.

Sam Barton knocked on his door just as he was taking a sip of his espresso. Waving him into a chair, Alejandro scanned the document his lawyer pushed across the desk.

The letter, addressed to Clayton Hargrove, recapped the terms of the public apology the Salazar family was willing to accept from the Hargroves as compensation for the financial and reputational losses it had incurred as a result of the theft of its property.

Should the Salazars not receive a written response by the date indicated on the letter, the family would proceed with its plans to prosecute the Hargroves to the fullest extent of the law, exposing the lies and criminal business practices the Hargrove dynasty had been built upon.

A very persuasive letter. Satisfied with its contents, Alejandro strengthened the language in a couple of sections, then pushed the document back across the desk to Sam.

His lawyer scanned the edits. Raised a brow. "That will get his attention."

"That's the point."

"And if he doesn't respond?"

"We cross that bridge when we come to it."

He was hoping that day never came. That Clayton Hargrove's lawyers would take the letter for the warning it was and advise their client accordingly. Because *this* had to end, this piece of history that was tearing his fiancée apart. This daily hope her father would call when the bastard clearly couldn't care less, because it was dismantling him too to see her this way.

It needed to be over.

Cecily resumed her life in New York determined to cultivate that unshakeable vision she had promised herself. She tuned out the newspapers and the gossip, focused on the future she and Alejandro were building together and refused to look back, only forward.

Controlled the things she could.

The week after they returned, their real estate agent found them a property in upstate New York that was everything they'd been looking for. Sitting in the shadow of the Catskill Mountains, Cherry Hill Farm, a two hundred and fifty acre spread being sold by its polo ground owners, was spectacular.

Cecily lost her heart to its scenic views across the Hudson Valley, acres of riding trails up into the mountains and its elegant, eighteenth-century ranch-style house.

"You love it," Alejandro said, flicking her a glance as they made the drive home after viewing it.

She nodded, excitement brimming inside her at the potential of such a special place. Warmer than the grand Esmerelda she'd grown up on, she knew it could be a wonderful home for her and Alejandro's family, plus a great base for her business. Something as special as La Reve.

And if that brought with it a host of questions as to where her relationship with Alejandro stood after that explosive night they'd shared together in Belgium, she ignored them just as she'd been doing all week.

She didn't want to examine the depth of feeling she had for him. How much she was coming to depend on him. The fact she'd unwisely allowed herself to care for a man who'd had no trouble playing by the rules ever since they'd returned to New York.

Maybe it was the way he made love to her with such passion, then walked away afterward as if he'd been untouched by it. As if he could turn his feelings off and on for her as he pleased while she felt as if the world was shifting beneath her feet. As if whatever brakes he'd been attempting to put on them that night in Belgium were firmly in place and he was keeping him there.

Or maybe it was because the very thing she'd been afraid of happening—that she would fall into love with him—was exactly what she'd done.

Bottom lip caught between her teeth, her attention was captured by the phone call Alejandro was having with their real estate agent. *Buying the farm.*

She gaped at him when he'd finished. "Did you just do that?"

"*Sim.* He was going to put it on the market tomorrow. Better not to take chances. Plus now we have a location for our wedding. We can get the invitations out."

Her stomach plummeted. Given the simple ceremony they'd envisioned and the wedding planner they'd hired to execute it for them, six weeks was more than enough time to execute it. It was not having it at Esmerelda that ripped open the jagged hole inside of her. The fact that there had still been no word from her father.

"*Don't,*" Alejandro murmured. "I am going to fix this, Cecily. I promise you."

How? Both sides were so deeply dug in, their pride ruling them, she didn't see any way around it.

She turned her head to stare out the window. Perhaps Alejandro had been right. Perhaps her father *would* see reason once he received their wedding invitation and acknowledged it as the inevitability it was. Because he wouldn't let her walk down the aisle without him, would he? As rocky as their relationship had been, she loved her father and deep down, she thought he loved her too.

* * *

Fortunately, she was too madly busy over the next few weeks to ruminate about anything except getting the renovations done at Cherry Hill Farm so the wedding could go on as planned.

The ceremony was to take place in the lovely wild flower garden at the back of the house, the reception, a barn party Alejandro had suggested as apropos for them. Which meant her priority was making sure the main barn—the showpiece of her new stables—was ready in time.

The days passed in a flurry of frenzied activity, a small army working at the farm. It was surreal, *magical,* to watch her dream come true. Her stomach swooped with butterflies every time she thought of saying her vows to Alejandro in the beautiful garden. Dancing her first dance with him under the sparkling Murano chandeliers inspired by La Reve.

If she worried she was committing herself to a man who might never love her, that those walls of his showed no signs of coming down, it was a reckless ride she couldn't seem to stop because he was becoming everything to her, this man who always kept his promises.

If she got too carried away, hot on its heels came the reminder her father had not yet responded to the deal Alejandro had offered him, nor to their wedding invitation. Neither had the better portion of the Hargrove clan for that matter—as if her father had orchestrated a family-wide boycott of their nuptials.

If this kept up, there would be only Salazars at her wedding.

It ate away at her insides, corroded her happiness. But she refused to show it.

An unshakeable vision.

Two weeks before the wedding, she arrived home well after dinner, so exhausted she could hardly move, but bubbling over with enthusiasm with the progress of the day. Curled up in the chair beside Alejandro's desk, she gave him a recap.

"It sounds as if you're almost there," he said, leaning back in his chair, coffee cup in hand.

"We are. It's going to be amazing." She set her gaze on the man who seemed intent on doing everything he could to help her rebuild her life alongside his. "Thank you," she said huskily. "For this. For all of it."

He shook it off. "It's nothing. It's what I promised you."

"It's everything and you know it."

An enigmatic look claimed his face. He took a sip of his coffee, set the cup down. "I have to go to Colombia tomorrow."

"Colombia?" She blinked. "Our wedding is two weeks away. We have the ultrasound tomorrow."

"It's the acquisition…unavoidable, I'm afraid. I'll do the ultrasound, then leave for the airport from there."

"When will you be back?"

"Friday."

Friday. A week.

"Okay," she murmured, lifting her chin. She could hold down the fort for a week. She'd been doing it all along with his insane schedule.

They discussed a few urgent wedding items. She lost the plot somewhere along the way, her eyes drifting closed. Alejandro took her cup from her hand, placed it on the desk and pulled her to her feet.

"Bed," he instructed.

She stood on tiptoe, curved a palm around his nape and brought his mouth down to hers. "Come with me," she murmured against his lips, "and I will."

He pressed a hard kiss to her mouth. Set her away from him. "I have to get ready for this trip," he said quietly, "and you're dead on your feet. You should get some sleep."

Her skin stung. He'd hardly touched her over the past few weeks. She'd attributed it to the pressure he was under with this deal that was making the papers, the crazy amount of work he had on his plate. But she knew in that moment she hadn't been imagining the distance he'd put between them—it was a very real thing she'd been willfully avoiding. Testimony to his promise love wasn't ever going to be on offer from him even if he did feel something for her.

Too tired to face it now because she knew she was already in far too deep—she immersed herself in a long, hot bath, hating the hollow feeling inside of her. Hating that she'd come to need him so much.

Curling up in bed, she picked up her tablet. Eyes blurring, emotions too close to the surface, she checked her email before she turned out the light. Everything on track with the wedding, she flipped to their RSVP inbox. Froze at the email from her father.

She pressed a shaking finger to the screen to open it. It wasn't from her father, it was from his assistant, Claire.

Your father regrets to inform you he will not be able to attend your wedding.

No explanation. No elaboration. He hadn't even sent it himself.

A tear slipped down her cheek. Then another, until they were a steady, inexorable flow.

She had to go see him. She had to know the truth.

She and Alejandro attended the ultrasound together the next morning at her doctor's plush Upper East Side clinic. Everything thankfully on track, their baby healthy and thriving with a vibrant heartbeat, Cecily found herself left with a remarkable sonogram and a whole host of emotions after her fiancé departed for the airport.

Anticipation about her and Alejandro's baby had replaced fear as her dominant emotion as she put her faith in the future. With it had come a desperately strong hope her baby would be a girl—that she would develop that same unbreakable bond with her child that she'd had with her mother and maybe it would fill some of the void still left inside of her.

She flew to Kentucky the day before Alejandro was due home, the finishing touches on the barn almost complete, last-minute wedding tasks in her planner's capable hands. Cliff, bless his heart, met her at the airport.

She gave him a hug. "Thank you for coming."

"It was a good escape for me. How is New York treating you?"

"Just fine." She gave him a wary look as she drew back. "How's father?"

"Missing you," he said bluntly, "although he refuses to admit it. The place hasn't been the same without you."

"Kay?" She wrinkled her nose to hide the sharp stroke of pain that cut through her. "Left to her own devices, she'll spoil everything."

"Yes," Cliff said with meaning. *"Kay."*

They drove out to the farm. The familiar lush beauty of Kentucky's horse country hit her like a brick to the chest. *How had she survived without this?*

A vision of Cherry Hill Farm with its spectacular canopy of pink cherry blossoms and soaring views up into the mountains filled her head. *That* was why. Because she wanted that life she'd envisioned with Alejandro so badly it hurt.

She gave into the impulse to go see her horses when they arrived, which didn't help her level of emotion as she rapped on the door of her father's study.

What if he wouldn't speak to her? What if he threw her out?

She let herself in at her father's curt command. He sat

behind the solid, cherry wood desk in a pose imprinted from childhood, head bent over the document he was reading, brow furrowed in concentration.

Swallowing past the lump that formed in her throat, she took in the newly imprinted lines bracketing his eyes and mouth as he looked up at her.

"Daddy."

His expression softened for a moment, a warmth entering his cool gray eyes, before his face closed over into an expressionless mask. "You didn't say you were coming."

She crossed her legs at the ankle, wrapped her arms tight around herself. "I got your RSVP. I wanted to talk to you."

"You made your choice, Cecily. You chose to marry a Salazar."

She pressed trembling lips together. "So your pride means more to you than I do?"

He rested his head against the back of the chair and regarded her with a hooded look. "I gave you everything… your career handed to you on a silver platter, the best coaches and horses in the world, every advantage you could ask for. You could have married a fine man like Knox, instead you chose to jump into bed with the man who is trying to destroy us. What do you want me to say?"

Her temper caught fire. She moved forward until she stood flush with the edge of the desk, hands clenched by her sides. "I would like you to care for me like a father should. And for the record, *I* made my career, not you."

An emotion she couldn't read flickered in those wintry gray eyes. "What I *want* from you, Daddy, is the truth. I want to know why you can't make this apology and put it behind us so I can be happy."

He got up from his chair and rounded the desk. "You think Alejandro is going to make you happy? He's marrying you to secure the Salazar you're carrying, Cecily.

He is *loving* taking you away from me, paying me back by stealing the one thing I value most, but he does not *love* you. Don't be so damn naïve."

Her insides curled into a tight little ball. "It was *me* who pursued Alejandro. And I do trust him. He's the only thing I *can* trust at the moment because you keep lying to me."

He gave her a stone-faced look. "Then you're being a fool."

She swung away to the window, a wet heat blurring her eyes as she stared out at the perfectly manicured gardens. She blinked the tears back, fighting the show of emotion, but they fell unbidden down her cheeks.

"Cecily," her father rasped, placing a hand on her shoulder. "You're making me make impossible decisions."

"Why?" She swung around. *"Tell me why* so I understand."

He raked a hand through his hair. Rested a palm on the window ledge. "My father, in a severe lapse in judgment, made a deal with Paul Macintosh to stud Diablo to Demeter while Diablo was on loan to him. Your grandmother, as you know, was obsessed with beating Adriana, convinced if she had a horse as good as Diablo she could. So my father made it happen. No one was ever supposed to know."

"But the groom talked."

He frowned. "How do you know about him?"

"Adriana told me. She said we bought him off."

"Unfortunately, yes. My mother was terrified of what would happen to her career if anyone found out…that she could be blacklisted or worse, stripped of her titles. So my father paid him off."

"How did you know about it?"

"The groom came back years later, short on money, threatening to spill the story. I gave him more money hoping that would be the end of it."

"But it wasn't." She bit the inside of her mouth. "Was

that what you were arguing with mother about the day she died?"

"Yes." The single word dismantled her insides. "I thought it was better she didn't know. That *neither* of you knew. That you focused on your careers." He shook his head, eyes bleak. "In hindsight, I should have known it was the wrong thing to do. Your mother was so emotional. She'd built her career on those horses. It was," he said heavily, "my fault."

Her heart pulled loose, anger and confusion clawing at her insides. All these years she'd wondered why her father couldn't love her the way she needed him to...why the aloofness he had always carried had suddenly grown so much deeper, when it had been guilt driving him all along.

"I was trying to protect you," he said quietly, eyes on hers. "I've always been trying to protect you, Cecily, to do what's best for you, even when it hasn't always appeared that way."

She got that. She even believed it. But she wasn't sure she could forgive him for sending her mother off in emotional distress while he went and did business in New York. For taking away her best friend.

Heat flashed in her father's eyes. "Don't you think I wish I'd done things differently? I miss her too, Cecily. Every single day. But I can't change history. It's the one thing I *can't* do."

Her nails dug into her palms. "You could apologize."

"A public apology would stain your grandmother and mother's reputation. *Yours*. Dismantle everything we've built. I won't break the promises I've made."

Even if he broke her heart keeping them.

She pressed her palms to her temples. "The Salazars will level you. Alejandro is a powerful man, Daddy. He's not just going to walk away from this."

Her father's mouth thinned. "He's made that clear. Perhaps you should remember that yourself. He *is* ruthless, Cecily. Have you read the letter he sent?"

What letter?

He walked to his desk, came back with a piece of paper he handed to her. She skimmed the letter. The last paragraph sucked the breath from her lungs.

Should you not respond to this communication by the date indicated, expressing the Hargrove family's intent to make the public apology outlined above, the Salazar family will proceed with its plans to prosecute to the fullest extent of the law, exposing the lies and criminal business practices the Hargrove dynasty has been built upon.

The blood drained from her face. She'd thought it would never come to this. She'd thought her father would make the apology. And perhaps, she acknowledged grimly, she'd thought Alejandro might bend given the growing feelings between them. *Because she didn't think he would do this to her.*

Her father trained his gaze on hers. "You think you know him, Cecily…that you can *trust* him…that he *cares* for you? Tell him to back off…to leave ancient history where it belongs."

CHAPTER THIRTEEN

ALEJANDRO ARRIVED HOME late on Thursday evening, his Colombian acquisition complete. He'd left the post-deal celebrations to his legal team and flown on to Kentucky in an effort to talk some sense into Clayton Hargrove, only to have a series of thunderstorms send him home instead.

Unfortunate with his wedding a week away and his schedule jam-packed. But he'd also been anxious to get home to Cecily. She hadn't sounded right on the phone when he'd talked to her last night—hadn't sounded right all week.

He knew he'd hurt her before he'd left, but giving in to his weakness for her, allowing their relationship to slide back into what it had been was not something he was going to do—not now when they'd developed exactly the kind of safe, solid partnership he'd been looking for. Knowing a confrontation with her father was on the horizon had also been extra incentive to keep his head clear.

Dropping his briefcase in the living room, he shrugged off his jacket and flicked on a light. Cecily must still be up at the farm. He poured himself a drink and wandered over to the floor-to-ceiling windows to take in a floodlit view of Central Park while he waited for her.

He'd been giving Clayton Hargrove time to come around—*to do the right thing*—so he didn't have to make decisions he didn't want to make. To choose between the two loyalties rapidly tearing him apart. But Clayton had backed him into a corner instead.

He couldn't ask his grandmother to give anymore than she already had. His only remaining option was to call

Clayton's bluff, a card he was loathe to play given what he really wanted was Cecily's father at the damn wedding.

Twenty minutes passed. Thirty. Visions of Cecily stranded by the side of a busy highway filled his head. He had put down his empty glass, was about to call her and give her hell for not texting she'd be late when she walked through the door.

His senses settling, he crossed to greet her. Setting his hands on her waist, he bent to kiss her, but she turned her cheek at the last minute, the kiss landing on her jaw. He frowned and set her away from him. Surveyed her pale face and stiff demeanor. "What's going on?"

She threw her purse on a chair. "I flew to Kentucky yesterday to speak with my father."

Meu Deus. He'd been hoping to get to him first. "Why didn't you tell me?"

"Because I was trying to handle it myself." Her gaze was a wintry blue as she trained it on him. "Because *you* told me once that I'm in charge of my own happiness, so I went to him to get the answers I was looking for."

And they hadn't been the ones she wanted. "What did he say?"

"He told me the truth. That my grandfather did what we all think he did. That it was a mistake he's been covering up ever since in order to preserve the legacy of three careers."

"Is that what your parents were arguing about the day your mother died?"

She nodded. "The groom showed up the night before asking for more money. My mother was terrified it would ruin her career when she found out."

"At least you know she wasn't keeping it from you."

"But it was unnecessary," she bit out, mouth trembling. "All of it. If my father had told my mother the truth, if she hadn't been so upset that day, it never would have happened."

"You can't know that," he murmured, brushing a thumb across her cheek. "Your father isn't responsible for your mother's death, Cecily. No one is. I know how much you loved her, what a special bond you had, but she's gone. You need to let her go."

"I do," she agreed, fire glinting in her eyes, "and so do you. This *devastation*," she said, waving a hand at him, "this badly miscalculated mistake my grandfather made—it needs to end, Alejandro."

"Tell your father to apologize and it will."

"He won't do it. He promised my grandmother and my mother he would never sully their legacies. He'd rather you strip him of every cent he has than break his promise."

He clenched his hands by his sides. "So he elects to use you as a pawn instead? He knows exactly what he is doing, Cecily. By putting you squarely in the middle, by tearing my loyalties in two, he won't have to sacrifice anything. It's the same insane arrogance your family has been perpetuating for decades."

"Funny," she said quietly, "that's what he said about you. That *I* am *your* power play. That you are only marrying me to secure your heir…that you are enjoying taking away the one thing he values most."

"That's ridiculous," he bit out. "You know what you mean to me."

"I thought I did." Turbulent emotion swirled in those blue eyes. "Now I'm not so sure."

He narrowed his gaze. "Explain."

"My father showed me the letter you sent him. You were supposed to be getting him to see reason, Alejandro, not threatening to annihilate him."

That made his skin sting. "I *gave* him time to see reason. I *hand delivered* him a generous compromise—a much more generous one than most would offer. I was on my way to talk sense into him today when my flight was diverted—time I don't have. But sometimes, *querida*, the only thing a man like him understands is the bottom line."

"And that worked well didn't it? You are like two stags engaged in a fight to the finish. There will be no winner in this."

He threw up his hands. "What would you have me do?"

"Drop this," she said quietly. "We can heal this wound together if we refuse to perpetuate it. You said so yourself when you first proposed marriage."

"That was assuming your father was a reasonable man."

She regarded him silently. "Is it really so different what he is doing than what you are? He is trying to preserve my family's honor just as you are yours."

"A crime was committed, that is the *difference*," he growled. "Don't make me make impossible decisions, Cecily."

Exactly what her father had said. Cecily turned away, arms wrapped around herself, feeling like a patchwork quilt she was knitted into so many pieces, the stitches barely holding.

She'd left Kentucky battered and broken over her father's refusal to *choose her* over a decades-old feud. Over the realization his love and duty toward her mother, something that had always been so passionately strong, had superseded his feelings for her. But it had also answered the question she'd asked herself at the very beginning of her and Alejandro's relationship.

"Cecily?" Alejandro curved his fingers around her arm and turned her back to him.

She lifted her gaze to the frustration tangling in his. "I thought I could do it," she said huskily. "A practical marriage to you for the sake of our child. I thought that what we could have together was better than this secret desire I've always had to be loved, because who knew if that even existed for me?

"And then," she said, taking a deep breath, "you made me believe in *you*. You were the one thing in all of this I could hold on to when everything else was crumbling beneath my feet. You were my *person*."

His gaze darkened. "I still am. That hasn't changed."

"No," she agreed. "*I've* changed. I allowed myself to fall in love with you. I started buying into this dream we were building together and once I started, I couldn't stop. I want it all, Alejandro. I want that unconditional love we talked about that night at La Reve. I want you to *choose me* over this feud that is tearing us all apart."

He looked as if he'd been sucker punched. "I did choose you. I'm marrying you. We are building a life together."

"No," she said, "you're marrying me because I'm carrying your child. And maybe because on some level you care for me, because I believe you do. But ours will never be a real marriage. You will never let yourself love because your past has made you too afraid to do it."

His face shuttered. "I'm not *afraid* to love, I *refuse* to go there because I know it will mess up a perfectly good relationship. Because we have more to consider in this than just us—we have a child on the way."

She shook her head. "Allowing yourself to feel won't mess *us* up. It will make us *better*."

"It's inconsequential," he said curtly. "Love is not a capacity I have, Cecily. I've been clear about that from the beginning. I'm not trying to be obstinate, I'm telling you the truth."

Her heart dropped at the utterly closed off look on his face. *She'd known this was coming, hadn't she?* That she'd been letting her feelings run away with her in the hope the caring she sensed in him might turn into the love she needed. The love she now knew she *deserve*d. But to hear him say it, to reject it so completely, was like a knife to the insides.

"So what will you do?" she asked quietly. "Take my father to court? Put our child in the center of this war between two families, exactly what your parents did to you?"

"We will shield them from it," he rejected. "Ensure that never happens. Your father has a choice, Cecily, let him make it."

"So do you. You have the power to make this decision and yet you won't. *I* am expected to give up everything for a marriage with a man who will never love me."

His hands fisted by his sides. "Cecily—"

She swiped her purse off the chair. "I think we both need time to think."

"*About what?* We are getting married in a week."

"About whether I can do this. Because the man I fell in love with wouldn't do this to me. He wouldn't make me make this choice."

She turned and stalked to the door. He followed, his face a dark cloud. "Stay and we'll talk this out. You can't just walk off into the night like this. You're clearly emotional."

She pivoted to face him, eyes flashing. "I am *emotional,* Alejandro. So give me the space I'm asking for."

"Where will you go?"

"I have no idea." She yanked the door open before that last stitch gave. "Given the two males in my life have managed to so thoroughly disappoint me, I feel the need for some distance."

Gluing his feet to the floor, Alejandro resisted the urge to go after her. It might push her over the edge in the mood she was in. But the thought of her out there alone in New York, even with his credit cards, made him crazy.

He traced a path back to the bar instead and poured

himself another glass of Scotch, his fury growing with every breath. She couldn't just change the rules of the game at the eleventh hour. *Decide* she loved him, then walk away. Break the promises she'd made to him and his child.

Because as much as she'd enjoyed throwing his emotional unavailability at him, he had invested in her too…in this future they were building together. He had trusted her to stick—not to walk out that door in an eerily similar scene to one he'd been privy to far too many times in his life.

He collapsed in a chair. *I want it all, Alejandro. I want that unconditional love we talked about. I want you to choose me over this feud that is tearing us apart.*

He scowled at the amber liquid in his glass. *He* was the good guy here. He'd been honest about what he was capable of from the very beginning. It was Clayton Hargrove, the arrogant bastard, who was intent on breaking his daughter's heart.

He rested his head against the back of the chair. An envelope on the table caught his eye. Picking it up, he pulled out its contents. *The sonogram.* Living, breathing proof of the child he and Cecily had conceived together, it knocked the air from his lungs all over again.

It had all become too real. Too easy to envision the family he and Cecily could have together. How complete the idea of it made him feel. Tempting—too tempting to want to have it all—everything he'd never had.

Cecily made him want things he knew he couldn't have. He didn't have the inherent trust in him to subscribe to that kind of a vision—an unconditional love. He'd given that up a long time ago.

And hadn't she just proven his instincts right by walking out that door?

He woke the next morning with a viciously heavy head. Canceling his meetings, he flew to Belgium.

"I take it this isn't a social visit," his grandmother said over coffee the next morning on the porch, eyeing his combustible demeanor.

He shook his head and gave her the recap, finishing with Cecily's departure.

Adriana looked pensive. "What a mess," she murmured. "Can you really blame her? She feels as if she's been betrayed by the two men she loves."

"Yes," he bit out, "I can. You don't walk out on someone when you're having a disagreement. You talk it out. *Work* it out." He lifted a brow. "And who's side are you on anyway? This is *your* battle I've been fighting."

"Yes," she agreed softly, "and maybe Cecily's right. Maybe it's time it ended."

Blood pulsed against his temples. "You're telling me this *now?*"

His grandmother took a sip of her coffee. Sat back in her chair. "There's more to the story of Harper and I than you know. The rivalry we shared was epic, fueled by our mutual ambition. We pushed each other, made each other *better*. You might even have called us friends in the beginning. But somewhere along the way, it turned toxic, this need to win."

"Harper decided Diablo was the key to it all. When I wouldn't agree to allow her to stud him with Demeter, she lashed out, tried to hurt me. We were at a show in Barcelona when I discovered she was having an affair with your grandfather."

With Hugo? The most honorable man he'd known?

"It was a mistake," his grandmother acknowledged. "Harper was beautiful. *Irresistible* to men. And partly," she conceded, "it was my fault. My mindless obsession with my sport hurt your grandfather—he felt I loved it more than him at times. And maybe I did."

The remnants of a long-ago pain stained her dark eyes.

"The affair was over by the time I confronted him about it. I think he knew she had been using him. But it nearly cost us our marriage."

Alejandro attempted to absorb the chink in a relationship that had seemed bullet proof. "You forgave him."

"I loved him, so yes I did. Marriage is never perfect, Alejandro. It's messy and complex, but your grandfather and I built something strong enough that it withstood the difficult times. He was the love of my life."

He took a sip of his coffee. Considered the message she was sending. He could have that with Cecily. He knew it in his heart. All he'd ever wanted from the beginning was to protect her—to take away the shadows. To *keep* her.

So why was it so hard to make that leap she was asking of him? Was the survival instinct that had driven him for so long simply too strong? And yet, he knew even as he thought it, that he loved her. That she'd found a way beneath those defenses of his from the very beginning until she'd crawled into the very heart of him.

He'd spent every minute since denying what he knew to be true because she made him feel so alive, so complete, he couldn't contemplate ever losing her.

Except where had that gotten him? He would lose her now if he wasn't careful.

His grandmother set a gnarled, weathered hand on his. "Go find Cecily. Tell her it's over. I've spent far too much time and emotion chasing my pride, Alejandro. Enough is enough."

He nodded. "I'll go talk to Clayton."

"No," Adriana said, fixing her dark gaze on him. "Leave Clayton to me."

CHAPTER FOURTEEN

ALEJANDRO RETURNED TO New York intent on finding Cecily and making things right. Except his fiancée had turned her phone off and wasn't returning his calls.

She was not, according to her father, in Kentucky, apparently having followed through on her vow to achieve distance from both of them. Nor was she in Manhattan according to the private detective who'd worked on the Hargrove file for him. Which left him precisely nowhere—five days before his wedding.

The calls started then. First the wedding planner with one urgent item after another, then the contractors at the farm with some last minute snags on the finishing materials. With no capacity to sit on a phone all day advising them on things he couldn't see, he moved up to the Cherry Hill and managed his business from there.

His fiancée would, he assumed, come talk to him when she was ready. *Which needed to be soon.*

He personally supervised the unloading of Cecily's horses as they arrived from Kentucky—his other surprise for her. He even went out and bought a box of that crazy-looking American cereal for Bacchus who was now missing home as well as his mistress.

He could identify. A piece of Cecily haunted him everywhere he looked. Taunting him with his own stupidity—reminding him of what he stood to lose.

He woke the next morning to a text from Cecily saying she was fine. That she needed more time to think. No clue to her whereabouts. No time frame on the thinking.

He left another message for her. Told her he needed to talk to her. No reply.

Was she trying to make him sweat? Or was she recon-sidering marrying him?

And then it was the day before his wedding. All the renovations complete, the main barn a gleaming master-piece of wrought-iron and mahogany, he wrote a massive check to the construction manager and thanked him and his team for their hard work.

Watching them leave, a very real fear consumed him that Cecily wasn't coming back. That he had hurt her so badly by not putting her first, by letting her down like everyone else, he'd ruined everything.

But she'd left him for God's sake. How the hell was he supposed to fix it if he was talking to himself?

"In case you've forgotten," Stavros drawled that evening in the Great Room at Cherry Hill, pool cue in hand, "a wedding does require a bride. You need to make a call on this, Salazar."

Alejandro was well aware of that. It was a fact his groomsmen had been dancing around all evening, but with two hundred guests set to descend here tomorrow, it was a reality he could no longer ignore.

"How about this?" Stavros suggested, lifting the cue. "I sink this shot, you call it off. I miss—we keep it in play for another twenty-four hours and hope she shows up for a *Concerto in E*."

Antonio grimaced. "This is no time for your warped sense of humor."

"On the contrary," the Greek drawled, "some humor is desperately needed here."

"Not that kind," Sebastien interjected. "Maybe we should determine what we're going to tell the guests if we do call it off."

"A permit issue with the renovations," Antonio sug-gested.

"Not bad," Sebastien pondered thoughtfully.

"Or you could call it off *now*," Stavros said. "Before half of New York gets into their cars and drives up here."

If he were smart, Alejandro conceded, that's what he would do. But he had signed on for this future he and Cecily had built together. He had promised to never let her down. *He* wasn't going to be the one to bail on her.

"I'll make a decision in the morning."

Cecily paced the veranda of the rustic cabin she'd rented in the Catskills as the sun made its way into the sky.

Her wedding day.

Her heart climbed into her mouth. She had to make a decision. She was supposed to marry Alejandro in hours. But nothing seemed clear.

This idyllic paradise, buried deep in the heart of the mountains had seemed the perfect place to think. *To lick her wounds.* Because both her father and Alejandro had cut her deeply.

She knew it was Alejandro's sense of honor at work, knew her history was at play here too, but she wanted, *needed* that unconditional love from the man she married. She couldn't settle for less.

And yet, she conceded, leaning against the pillar of the veranda and looking out at the splendor of the red and gold leaves, all this beautiful place had done was remind her of the home she and Alejandro were building—the place where her heart was.

And so—her impossible decision. Marry Alejandro and grow to hate him for what he was doing to her family. To *her*. Don't marry him and deprive her child of a home and herself of the man she loved.

She watched the sun rise high above the trees. A long-ago conversation with her mother filtered through her head. *"You don't choose who you love, Cecily. How and when you love. You just do."*

Something unraveled inside her. And suddenly she knew.

The yard at Cherry Hill was a beehive of activity as Cecily pulled the car into the parking lot.

She sat in the car and watched it all flow by, fear gripping her bones. What if Alejandro hated her for doing this to him? What if he didn't want to marry her now?

Paralyzed, she sat there until the wedding planner, Mariana, flew by in a panic. Pulse pounding in her throat, she stepped from the car.

The morning sunlight lit the façade of the main barn. *Her vision come to life.* But there was something new—a sign the crew had affixed above the main doors.

Hargrove-Salazar.

A knot tied itself in her throat. Her feet moved without conscious decision, carrying her through the massive mahogany doors. The whicker of a horse greeted her, then a frenzied whinny and a stamping of feet.

Bacchus. She flew across the cobblestoned floor, fumbled with the latch on the door of his box and stepped inside, throwing her arms around his neck.

Had her father relented?

Deciding he'd received enough love, Bacchus nuzzled her pockets. She laughed. "I'm sorry. I don't have any right now."

"There's a box of your scary-looking American cereal in the feed room," Alejandro said quietly.

Her heart thumped against her chest. She turned to find him standing outside Bacchus's box. He looked so gorgeous in dark jeans and a white T-shirt, his hair mussed beyond redemption, she ached to throw herself in his arms. But she didn't because he also looked mad. *Furious*.

"I was coming to see you."

"And you left it until *now?*" He shook his head, fire lighting his eyes. "You left the ball in my court, Cecily. How the hell was I supposed to respond if I couldn't find you?"

She crossed her arms over her chest, stomach sinking. "I needed time to think. You are a force of nature. I was worried if I let you in, you would steamroll me into making a decision I wasn't ready to make."

He rested a palm against the stall door. "So have you?"

She stepped out of the box and latched the door. Braved all that suppressed male fury as she stepped into his space. "Yes," she said, lifting her gaze to his. "I love you, Alejandro. We are going to find a way to make this work."

A flicker of something in those dark eyes—the faintest softening she hoped might be a positive sign. He caught her hand in his and tugged her closer until all she could feel was the heat vibrating from him.

"I have some things to say to you too," he said huskily, eyes on hers. "First of all, I let you down, Cecily. I promised you I would always be there for you—that I would make this right and I didn't. That will never happen again.

"Secondly, Adriana went to Kentucky to see your father. It's over, this feud between the Salazars and the Hargroves. Your father and Kay are here for the wedding."

Her father was here? Adriana had gone to Kentucky? Her head spun. "What happened between them?"

"I have no idea and I don't care. Thirdly," he said eyes on hers, "I chose *you* the night I crossed the line and made love to you at Esmerelda. I chose you when I asked you to marry me. I chose *you* the night you gave me that damn speech about unconditional love." He brushed a thumb across her cheek. "You break my heart, *querida*. You always have."

Her breath caught in her chest. "What are you saying?"

"That I love you. I fell in love with you that night in Belgium, Cecily. That's why I pulled away. Because nothing good in my life has ever lasted. I couldn't stand for that to happen to us."

Her heart leaped in her chest. "It won't," she said fiercely, cupping his jaw in her hands. "What we have is special, Alejandro. *Powerful.* Look what we've done... we've ended the longest-running feud in equine history."

A smile curved his lips. "I want to chase this dream with you," he said softly. "I want that unconditional love you talked about. But I am not perfect. I'm going to have my moments. Which doesn't mean I won't always be there for you because I will."

That completely undid her. Throat too thick to speak, she grabbed a handful of his shirt, stood on tiptoe and kissed him—a sweet, shimmering, soul affirming kiss that promised forever.

The hint of uncertainty in his eyes as he drew back made her frown. "What is it?"

"I thought I might have ruined it."

She melted. "You can't ruin love, Alejandro. It just is."

It wasn't something he was going to accept overnight. It was going to take time. Luckily she had the rest of her life to prove it to him.

The afternoon dawned a picture-perfect, unseasonably warm, fall day in the Catskills—as if some higher power had decided Cecily and Alejandro had already defeated enough of the elements and today was reserved for the bright, shiny future they would have.

Her elegant chignon in place, the stylist slipped Cecily's romantic, spaghetti-strapped, ballerina-style dress over her head, the gown settling over her hips in a whoosh of silk. With its elaborate, scalloped bodice, plunging back and floral embroidered lace overlay, the only adornment required were her mother's drop sapphire earrings.

That final grounding element in place, she descended the central staircase of the ranch house to where her father stood waiting at the bottom.

A flash of emotion stained his gray eyes as she took his arm. "You look beautiful."

"Thank you."

He frowned. "Cecily—"

She shook her head. "This is the beginning of a new chapter, Daddy. We decide where it goes from here."

He was silent for a moment, then nodded, walking her outside into the sunshine.

Somehow Alejandro had managed to keep the hordes of photographers circling the estate via helicopter away from the private affair they had wanted it to be. Cecily ignored the distraction as she entered the garden on her father's arm, the fall blooms a riot of red and gold around them. Her focus was firmly on the man who waited for her at the end of the aisle, a look of pure possession on his face.

Alejandro's three groomsmen, Stavros, Antonio and Sebastien all looked devastatingly handsome in dark suits and silver ties, but Alejandro was the only man who would ever make her heart beat this way—as if her whole world revolved around him.

Stavros gave a low whistle, eyes on Alejandro's bride. "Well I'd say she's worth the merry tune she has you dancing."

Antonio eyed him. "And you aren't dancing one yourself?"

Stavros lifted a shoulder as if to concede the point since

everyone knew he was mad about his so called 'convenient wife'. "Salazar, however, is *love struck*."

Well, yes he was. But Alejandro wasn't fighting it anymore. Not when he'd almost lost the woman who had come to mean everything to him. He kept his eyes on Cecily as she negotiated the long row of seats on her father's arm to the strains of a classical Bach piece. And then suddenly she was there by his side, her father giving her away.

He brushed a kiss against her cheek. "You okay?" he murmured. "You look very focused."

Her lips curved in a winsome smile. "Yes."

"Marry me then."

And so she did.

"Well that's the last man down," Stavros concluded, saluting Alejandro with his beer as the barn party moved into full swing. "You must be feeling good about yourself," he said to Sebastien.

The Englishman lifted a shoulder. "It's good to see you three happy."

"A toast then," Alejandro said, tipping his glass toward Sadie, Calli, Monika and Cecily who looked up to no good whispering at one of the tables. "To the women in our lives and our luck in finding them."

The men lifted their glasses in a salute and drank, all of them, Alejandro was sure, aware of how lucky they were.

"Apologies," Stavros said to Sebastien when he'd lowered his glass, "that Alejandro and I can't make the press conference on Monday. It's an admirable thing you're doing, Sebastien, giving away half your net worth."

"You're forgiven," Sebastien allowed, "since I've put you all on the Rapid Response board of directors."

"Oh, no," said Stavros, lifting his hands. "No bandwidth here."

"Me neither," said Alejandro.

Antonio frowned. "Yeah, I—"

"Excuse me." Mariana arrived to pluck Alejandro out of the group for the first dance. "I need him."

"Saved by the wedding planner," said Stavros.

"You have no capacity for that," Cecily observed as they waited for the band—*their* band from that night in Kentucky—to finish up the upbeat tune they were playing. "You have no time as it is. We're having a baby."

"I know," he said, lacing his fingers through hers. "But Sebastien tends to get what Sebastien wants."

The band introduced them to the crowd with a flourish. Cecily took Alejandro's hand and they walked onto the dance floor under the sparkling Murano chandeliers. A hand laced through his, the other on his shoulder, her head tucked under his chin, they danced to the same ballad they had that night in Kentucky.

Time fell away and suddenly she was back under that star-filled sky, dancing with the man she'd fallen madly in love with. Except this time, it wasn't just for one night—it was for forever.

"Alejandro," she murmured.

"Mmm?"

"It's not my song anymore. I *got* everything I wanted. Well," she added, a wistful note to her voice, "almost everything."

He leaned down to kiss her. "You will have that too. Remember the rule?"

An unshakeable vision.

EPILOGUE

World Championships of Show Jumping, Normandy, France.

VIRGINIA NELISSEN GALLOPED out of the stadium having compiled four faults in a lightning-fast round that had the Dutch team sitting in first place with only the last American rider to go.

"Boo," said Alejandro to his eighteen-month-old daughter, Zara Rose, sitting on his lap with a front row seat to the action. "We don't like her. She was mean to Mama."

"Boo," said Zara, imitating his scowl.

"Excelente," he murmured, pressing a kiss to the top of her head. "Now," he whispered as Cecily cantered into the ring, "you have to cheer for team Hargrove-Salazar. Because *this* is going to make history."

"Salazar-Hargrove," Adriana corrected tartly. "And I really don't like how nervous Cecily is. She was wrapping enough fences in the warm up to bring the whole course down."

Because this was his wife's dream. Because ever since her return to riding she'd been anchoring the American team on Socrates and been brilliant while doing it.

If there was pressure here today, it was on the woman riding into the ring, hair caught up in a sleek chignon beneath her velvet helmet, navy coat and crisp white shirt perfectly pressed. But if there was anything he knew about his wife by now, it was that she was a fighter. A survivor. She would leave it all in the ring today.

Cecily brought Socrates to a halt in front of the judges

and took off her hat in a salute. The applause and buzz of the crowd died down until you could hear a pin drop in the stadium. And then there was only the sound of Socrates's hooves pounding the sand as Cecily pushed him into an easy canter with a touch of her heels to his sides.

His smooth, glorious stride ate up the ground as Cecily guided him to the first jump, a high, complicated juxtaposition of poles Socrates eyed as unfamiliar then proceeded to rap hard as he cleared it.

Not an auspicious start. Adriana was right—both rider and horse were nervous.

An easy turn to the next jump and Socrates was taking off too late, clearing the jump by the skin of his teeth, then roaring toward the next, where Cecily placed him at the jump too early, forcing him to exert a superhuman effort to make it to the other side unscathed.

"Lord have mercy," said his grandmother, covering her eyes. "I can't watch."

A nice long gallop to the next oxer, he watched Cecily visibly collect herself and her horse. *Good.* They cleared the wide, imposing jump with perfect form. Then it was a quick turn to the triple combination that had felled every single rider thus far including Virginia, the jumps trickily placed off-stride to test the riders.

Cecily attacked it with military precision, placing Socrates perfectly for the first jump, then sailing over the next two with shortened strides that efficiently addressed the challenge.

His wife glanced at the clock with four jumps to go. She was close to time faults. She needed to avoid them and go clear for the American team to win. His stomach dropped as Cecily whipped Socrates around at a near suicidal angle and galloped toward the next combination at a speed that made Adriana gasp.

"Dear God," she said. "That's a bad call—that's—"

Socrates whipped over the first jump, galloped flat out toward the second and annihilated it too.

"—brilliant," said his grandmother.

She's retiring, thought Alejandro.

A sharp turn to the right and his wife was thundering toward the last jump. The crowd was on its feet now, caught up in the gutsy ride, its home team already out of it.

One more jump, Alejandro whispered. *One more jump, angel, you can do it.*

And then she did.

Cecily rode into the collecting ring where the media was assembled for the post competition interviews.

She had nothing left for them. Had gone through every facet of the emotional spectrum out there on that course, her mother's riding pin attached to her chest. When she caught sight of Alejandro waiting for her, Zara in his arms, a sob rose to her throat.

Her husband set Zara down. Cecily kicked her feet out of the stirrups and slid off Socrates's back and into his arms—the man who had never failed to catch her each and every time she'd stumbled over the past year: as she'd become a new mother, as she'd resumed her career, as she'd walked the tenuous road of balancing both.

Alejandro cupped her jaw and kissed her. "No tears, *meu carinho*. You were magnificent. Your mother would be so proud."

The tears came then in a great big flood. For the things she'd lost. For the things she'd gained. For what was still ahead.

A reporter from an American sports network descended on them, noting Adriana's legendary presence. "Perfect.

Can I have an interview with the complete team Hargrove-Salazar then?"

"Team Salazar-Hargrove," Adriana corrected. "And yes you may."

* * * * *

If you enjoyed Jennifer Hayward's contribution to
THE SECRET BILLIONAIRES *trilogy*
don't forget to read the first two stories

DI MARCELLO'S SECRET SON
by Rachael Thomas

XENAKIS'S CONVENIENT BRIDE
by Dani Collins

Available now!

MILLS & BOON®

MODERN™

POWER, PASSION AND IRRESISTIBLE TEMPTATION

A sneak peek at next month's titles...

In stores from 13th July 2017:

- **An Heir Made in the Marriage Bed** – Anne Mather
- **Protecting His Defiant Innocent** – Michelle Smart
- **The Secret He Must Claim** – Chantelle Shaw
- **A Ring for the Greek's Baby** – Melanie Milburne

In stores from 27th July 2017:

- **The Prince's Stolen Virgin** – Maisey Yates
- **Pregnant at Acosta's Demand** – Maya Blake
- **Carrying the Spaniard's Child** – Jennie Lucas
- **Bought for the Billionaire's Revenge** – Clare Connelly

Just can't wait?
Buy our books online before they hit the shops!
www.millsandboon.co.uk

Also available as eBooks.

0717/01